Fatal Flaws

"An unhappy trial attorney. A biased judge. An egocentric big-firm lawyer. And a group of deceitful doctors. Sound familiar?......These are just some of the characters brought to life on the pages of a new book by Boston attorney James P. McCarthy." "Fatal Flaws is the tale of a young, frustrated attorney going up against the establishment – a pedigreed big-firm attorney who went to the same Ivy League school as the trial judge, and the almighty HMOs – to find justice for a 13-year-old girl dying of kidney disease." "a classic David vs. Goliath type struggle."

- Massachusetts Lawyers Weekly

"**Fatal Flaws** depicts the trials and tribulations of pursuing accountability for medical malpractice which affects millions of Americans." "According to Mark Twain, '*The only difference between fiction and non-fiction is that fiction should be completely believable.*' Author Attorney McCarthy has challenged the system by exposing its *Fatal Flaws* and should be commended for his contribution to those who don't have a voice."

- Linda DeBenedictis, President and Founder, New England Patients' Rights Group

Fatal Flaws is a "medical malpractice drama"…"represents the world of the courtroom through the eyes of the victim"…"mercurial courtroom scenes".

- Boston Sunday Globe

"The new Boston-based medical malpractice thriller, 'Fatal Flaws' is about a young lawyer representing a little girl hospitalized for kidney problems. Complications ensue. Small firm lawyer faces lawyers from a big corporate law firm with vast resources. The book contains humor and confrontation. There's a twist at the end -- a fatal flaw."

- The Beacon Hill Times

"Fatal Flaws, although the book is fiction, is certainly a snapshot of the real world of medical malpractice litigation. The story is fast moving, the characters believable and the courtroom drama is certainly realistic. This could only have been accomplished by someone of your experience and talent. The book dissects a medical malpractice trial in a fictionalized tale with real world lessons. You have written a novel that both entertains and teaches."

- Paul R. Sugarman, Esq.
Former Dean of Suffolk Law
School and Former President of
Mass. Academy of Trial Lawyers

" I have been told that the writing and publication of a novel is similar to giving birth. Well, you have delivered. I found myself enmeshed in the story. The characters were people I knew, some likeable and others not so likeable. I 'knew' the lawyers having recognized them from my own experience, and we both know the judges as well as those invaluable clerks."

- John P. White, Jr., Esq.
Practicing Boston Trial Attorney

"To know even one life has breathed
easier because you have lived. This
is to have succeeded."

Ralph Waldo Emerson

1/25/05

Paul:

Hope you enjoy reading
this Boston based
Medical Malpractice
courtroom thriller.
Many interesting courtroom
clashes.

Enjoy

Jim

James P. McCarthy practices law in Boston, Massachusetts, and has been an active medical malpractice attorney for over thirty years.

Acknowledgments

Special thanks to Marilyn Weller for her patient assistance, incisive editing and invaluable insight. Marilyn made my writing of *Fatal Flaws* an extremely positive and invaluable experience. I am also very grateful to Paula Ronan for her thoughtful insight and her great patience in typing my endless revisions. I also extend special thanks and gratitude to Judy Gennochio, Lisa and Paulo Moura, Hans Ikier, Les Bloomenthal, Richard Shea, Edward McNeely and Walter Connolly.

To my wife, Mary, the joy and love of my life.

Fatal Flaws

Copyright   © 2003 by James P. McCarthy
All rights reserved

First printing 2003.

Third printing 2005.

Cover designed by Erica Shultz

Library of Congress Control No.:   2002095945

ISBN Prefix No. and Decal: 0-9722925-0-0

PRINTED IN THE UNITED STATES OF AMERICA

10   9   8   7   6   5   4   3

To purchase additional copies of *Fatal Flaws*, contact Aihole Publishing Company, 219 Lewis Wharf, Boston, Mass. 02110 or fax orders to (617) 723-7484. Special discounts relating to large quantity sales and corporations, institutions, law school and charitable organizations. Visit our web site at www.fatalflaws.com.

Table of Contents

Chapter 1

The Beginning – Crossing the Bridge

The 6:00 A.M. traffic slowly built as Sean drove his aging station wagon across the Mystic River Bridge. The city of Boston never looked more beautiful than on this crisp sunny morning in mid October. The harbor islands were barely visible on the horizon. The early morning light struck Sean with a sudden warmth and he felt a surge of pure joy and exhilaration. Just for an instant, it looked like the world was his oyster and life could not be any more perfect.

As he carefully approached the awakening city on the down ramp, he casually caught sight of a lone freighter drifting slowly out to open sea beyond Castle Island. Sean felt a sudden yearning to be a passenger on that drifting freighter and to somehow escape his every-day world, but like a flash of lightning, reality intervened.

"Stop fantasizing!" he commanded himself, as he stole a glance at the frigate Constitution, "Old Ironsides," docked in the inner harbor. He was desperately trying to refrain from dreaming of happier times when his life was much simpler and his days much brighter. Oh how he wanted to return to those days, but why? Why did he want to escape? He should have been on top of the world.

Why was he so unhappy and gloomy? Wasn't he, in fact, one of the best medical attorneys in Boston? Didn't he work for one of the most prestigious small law firms in Boston? Hadn't he been very successful recently trying medical cases for the last eight months? Wasn't he a rising star on the trial scene? Could life be any better for him, his wife and two young children?

Sean listlessly weaved through mounting rush-hour traffic and he eventually turned sharply onto Tremont Street next to the Boston Common. Thoughts of his recent trial successes raced through his mind. He particularly was savoring the most recent success in Worcester and was still enjoying the joy of the all-night victory party which had taken its toll and made him a little fatigued and slightly hung over.

After parking at the Common garage, he strolled across the Boston Common and, instead of his customary practice of walking directly to his office, decided to pause and enjoy his surroundings. Meditating in the warm morning sun, he re-experienced his initial sense of warmth and clarity. He suddenly had an urge to chart his life and, as he stated, "to get his life in order" and somehow be a happier person.

Sean knew that, in reality, his life as a successful trial attorney was becoming unmanageable and was, in his mind, totally out of control. He felt he was running on a treadmill and he did not enjoy the fruits of his labor. He wondered, "Why, if I'm so successful in my work as a lawyer, is my life so unhappy? Why am I feeling so melancholy, depressed, confused? Why am I so sad? Is there something wrong with what I am doing?" As he watched the people walking though the Common, Sean truly envied their apparent joy and contentment. "Why are they so happy; Why am I so different?" Sean sat for more than an hour, glued to the bench. It took all his effort to lift himself up and to walk to the office. But, with heavy steps, he headed toward work, bracing himself to face the upcoming day's events, his dreaded reality.

*   *   *   *   *

Chapter 2

Life in the Fast Lane

The clatter of dancing feet greeted Sean. Roland and his gorgeous blonde secretary were practicing the latest Tango steps. Sean's thoughts jumped back to those he frequently had after hearing dancing feet at work: "What the hell is this law office all about? It this an Arthur Murray dance studio? a cocktail lounge? a Madison Avenue advertising firm? or a prominent Boston law firm?" Sean thought of the opposition, those who were always looking for an attorney's Achilles' heel. If they ever caught a glimpse of this, they would see how vulnerable the firm really was and how lightly and less intensely the firm prepared cases. He asked himself, "Who cares? We have great cases. I know how to prepare and try them. Why not enjoy the opportunity and go with the flow? If the ship starts sinking, I'll bail out and go to another firm, or start my own."

Sean knew, however, that he had few options to bail out. These days he was lucky to have a job in a busy law practice and fortunate to be the lead trial attorney in a small three-attorney firm. He vowed anew to count his blessings and do what he could with the cards he was dealt. Despite his deep foreboding, he always tried to be positive and optimistic and not allow negative thoughts to overwhelm him. Years ago, after he had graduated from law school, he spent an entire fall and winter seeking a position in any Boston firm. Sean remembered spending many hours simply meditating to quell his anxiety, and spending just as many hours working up the courage to approach an interview with an ivy league law firm. He found the interview experience terribly deflating and it nearly destroyed his self-confidence. Before each interview, he convinced himself that he knew he would not be accepted but was interviewing "for the experience." After a while, he learned how to accept rejection in good grace and not to become too discouraged. Sean frequently mixed meditation with soulful and earnest prayer and remembered a saying he had heard: "Success is failure turned inside out." He gave himself pep talks, especially saying "winners never quit" and constantly referred to positive sayings in order to keep up a good front and not lose his confidence. Back in the sixties, not too many Irish lawyers were welcomed at the Yankee State Street firms. He remembered in particular one annoying Harvard Law graduate, a junior partner with one of the best State Street firms, telling him coolly, "You went to all Jesuit institutions: Boston College High, Boston College,

Boston College Law School. You're one dimensional. Your resume has no diversification." Only later in his practice did Sean learn that being a so-called "triple Eagle" was not a sign of failure or a lack of diversification but a badge of honor and great distinction. The academic Jesuit schools that Sean had attended were, in fact, highly regarded and considered some of the best in the country.

He looked into Roland Murphy's well-appointed office. As usual, there were no law books or files on the desk. In fact, Roland had one of the cleanest desks in the city. Sean wondered when, or where, he actually did any legal work. The longer he stood there, the more the office began to look like an antique showroom rather than a law office. The only sign of legal activity appeared on the top of the desk where Roland had placed the shiny leather briefcase he carried with him at all times. Sean knew that it never contained any files. Roland, or as his friends called him "Rosie," bragged how he used it as a prop when he went to the bars because it impressed potential clients and referrals. "Clients always like lawyers who look busy," he would say. Rosie had a habit of losing these empty briefcases but it never bothered him; they were simply for show, not for substance nor for doing nightly legal work.

Sean walked to his office on the far side, figuratively miles away from the ornate conference room with a beautiful view of the Boston Common and the State House. Sean's office overlooked a high-rise that completely blocked his view of the city and the beautiful Boston skyline. When he looked out of his office window, he was faced with a brick wall. Whenever he stared out his window, deep in thought, he felt like he was looking out from a prison. He contrasted his "prison glimpse," as he would describe it, with Roland's extensive vista, which provided a panoramic view of the Boston Common, the golden dome of the State House, and the historic Park Street Church and Burial Grounds.

Quigley McPherson's office, directly across from Sean's, was another story. Sean walked over and looked in. There were pictures and statues of animals and birds everywhere. It looked like a zoo or a pigpen. The entire office was a disaster area strewn with yellow legal pads, files covering the floor, except there were none on the desk, clothing thrown around the room and umbrellas tossed in the corner. Pictures of his native Australia and his favorite hangout, London, were all over the place, and telephone messages were scattered across the desk. One's immediate impression was of someone working totally out of control, totally disorganized.

Sean thought the office suited Quigley to a tee, it spoke volumes about his lifestyle.

Sean's office was also cluttered, but it bore the marks of more organization and purpose. Case files lay on the desk and the floor, but they were aligned somewhat in order. Trial exhibits and courtroom charts littered the office but gave the look of a very busy and active trial lawyer. Here and there were the trappings of various trial exhibits, blow-ups of medical records, hospital documents, pictures of incubators, football helmets, anatomical and pathological blow-ups, skeletons, medical drawings, and charts. Sean enjoyed working amidst these exhibits from his trials because it gave him the taste and feel of the courtroom. In fact, he felt like his office was actually a mini courtroom, and he loved the smell and flavor of the exhibits because they inspired him to better prepare his cases. The sight of the exhibits gave him a certain exhilaration and sense of control, which he used to psyche him up for pending courtroom battles. His office also seemed to inspire his clients. They knew Sean was working diligently on their cases; clients like to think their lawyers are well-prepared.

The other secretaries would not arrive until 9:15 A.M. Everyone at MM&M usually came in on their own time schedule. The secretaries were also symbols of the 3M's hierarchy and its informal pecking order. Roland's secretary, Mary Jo, was a statuesque, very bleached blonde from Tennessee. This former head cheerleader had beautiful color and a charming southern accent. She looked gorgeous and dressed beautifully, a real Miss America, but she was not the fastest or most accurate typist. To add to her lack of office skills, she loved to chew gum and blow big sticky bubbles. This created a definite distraction from work. When she blew these bubbles, she didn't look particularly pretty, and the exploding gum tended to get stuck on her teeth and all over her face, especially when she was on the phone in animated conversation. Behind her back, Roland would say that Mary Jo, who was a beautiful adornment, made the office look pretty and served basically as an attractive woman to impress the male clientele and to give the office some class. Sean knew that Roland was an astute businessman and did not want to spend the real money it would cost to hire a professional secretary, someone who could actually type and spell.

Quigley's secretary, Bertha, a young and attractive brunette, was an excellent typist but she did not speak the King's English. Sean had to admit that it was fun listening to her on the phone as she mispronounced words and twisted her sentences.

They always sounded different and it was quite entertaining.

Sean's secretary, Jennifer, was a recent graduate of a local secretarial school and was still learning the finer points of typing briefs and motions. Jennifer, however, was extremely conscientious and more than made up for her inexperience and her typing mistakes by her dedication to her work. She was trustworthy and dependable. Sean was pleased with her work and she seemed to get along with everyone as well as making a favorable impression on his clients. She was very loyal to Sean and he trusted her implicitly.

As he went into his office and sat at his desk, he reflected on his life as a trial lawyer. It wasn't getting much easier. When he started out in the early sixties, he earned only $50 a week working for a parsimonious but brilliant trial attorney. He thought about the six-day weeks and the twelve-hour days and how he had been taken advantage of in his first position. Sean now knew that he had been ripped off by this lawyer from the beginning. He marveled, however, at how he had managed to parlay his early trial recognition and success into a way to meeting with Roland, a senior attorney, and how he had sufficiently impressed him, resulting in a position as "trial associate" on the letterhead of MM&M. And Roland had reason to be impressed. Sean had already started winning cases and, at that time, not too many trial attorneys in Boston were winning medical cases and obtaining verdicts.

Sean sat at his desk staring at the wall outside his dingy window. The dark environment lent itself to reflective thinking. Why he was so unhappy and dissatisfied? He should be on top of the world. But he knew why. He was practicing trial work with two seasoned rainmakers who were advancing their own interests and whose only goal in life was to get rich as quickly as possible. These crafty lawyers wanted to do as little trial work as possible. This is where Sean fit their bill and was useful to them. He was dedicated to his work and loved to try cases, while his associates, Rosie and Quigley, were dedicated to their pursuit of money and were constantly scooping up good cases. Their objective was to do no heavy lifting if at all possible, goals that were totally different from Sean's. Sean was highly idealistic, identified with his clients, and always viewed himself as an advocate for the underdog. Roland and Quigley were businessmen who merely wanted to make enough money so they could retire from law as soon as possible. Sean found their love of money and mercenary attitude less bearable with each passing day. He was thinking now of any way to escape their presence, to remove himself from the stifling legal plantation, his indenture and enslavement.

As he considered his options and ways to get out of this nightmare, he felt more and more trapped. He wondered how he would escape without endangering or destroying his family's fragile financial security. Sean was in a weak and insecure position. He did not have clients of his own and this made him vulnerable and put him at financial risk. As he sadly pondered his fate, he looked at the statue on his desk, a wounded Indian on a horse. Oh how he empathized with the dying broken Indian. He felt that his own love and dedication to law was slowly being strangled and would soon die if he did not change the course of his professional life. "But what can I do?" he desperately asked himself. "How can I get out of this mess? How can I change my life? Where can I go? What can I do?"

To calm himself, he thought more about the fate of the Native Americans. Sean loved their art and culture and identified with the struggles and tribulations of the Indians, who were so badly treated by the oppressive colonial forces and by the callous and deceitful US government. He wondered why he was fighting on the side of the arrogant unbending Boston establishment, while his heart identified with hopeless causes, the underdog, the deprived person, the minority. Sean glanced at the wood carving on top of his desk again. It had been given to him when he first started practicing law and the words imprinted on the wood always energized and inspired him. It was an old Indian expression: "Freedom and peace, behold them and always love them. They are sacred and you must treat them as such." The Indian's arms reached up to the heavens. Sean was now reaching and searching for his own freedom and peace. He knew that practicing law with Roland and Quigley was practicing law on the fast track. Sean knew he was on the fastest track of his life and if he didn't slow down soon, he was destined to end up in the breakdown lane. He was fearful not only for his family's financial stability but also for his own emotional, physical, and spiritual stability.

Sean, muttered to himself, "If only Roland and Quigley could change, our firm could be one of the best in the city." But, in his heart of hearts, he knew that they were creatures of habit and would never change. These two operators had spent a lifetime cruising the Boston bar scene and their bad habits were too ingrained.

Now, with the Worcester trial over, Sean was desperately trying to re-energize himself. The physical and mental strain of trying eight major medical cases in eight months had taken its toll.

Each case had lasted two to three weeks. He said to himself, "Too many, too soon." Sean had a string of successful verdicts and settlements but now his brain was fried and he was totally exhausted and burned out. Even though his family needed the extra money that any upcoming trials would harvest, he had to take a break. He could not physically or mentally continue at this pace, and he knew it.

Even though he would need to muster all his courage if he was to leave MM&M, Sean realized that this was the time for a major decision. He feared that if he continued on this current destructive pace, he would become a replica of Rosie and Quigley. Sean sensed that despite his best efforts, it was already happening, almost by osmosis. He was seeing too many familiar faces on his trips to the Boston bar scene and was now in danger of becoming part of it. He worried that he might be seen by his suburban neighbors which could ruin his reputation.

Sean knew that, to the world, MM&M looked extremely successful but, in actuality, the firm was on the brink of disaster. MM&M, he knew, was badly overextended and actually needed **more** trial lawyers not more cases. Sean could not do it all alone, but Roland and Quigley were basically too bottom line to hire another attorney. It would lower their personal profit and they simply didn't want to share their piece of the financial pie. Even though he was winning medical cases and getting great results, he was still receiving scraps for money. The day of reckoning would soon be at hand . He could not physically or mentally maintain this pace, trying one case after the other. He knew he had reached his limit, but Rosie and Quigley still insisted on marking up every medical case on the trial list like mad, hoping to force the other side to settle rather than go to a jury trial. But, these cases were no longer being settled, most were being tried.

Sean knew that the days of settling malpractice cases were over, but Rosie and Quigley weren't getting the message. The current defense psychology was to try every case right to the last day, right to verdict. The defense strategy was to wear down the plaintiff and the injured person with intense pre-trial discovery, costly depositions of all experts, and prolonged litigation to verdicts. This strategy also included flooding the media with anti-lawyer and anti-client barrages. The medical profession claimed that these lawsuits were not in the consumer's interest, but only led to higher medical and hospital costs. They tried to terrorize the public into believing that medical malpractice suits were bad for the quality of medical care and led to poorer, not better, quality of care. Over the past year or so, Sean had to challenge many potential jurors who claimed to be against suing a doctor because it would only increase the cost of their insurance premiums. Doctors had the public believing that if the lawsuits continued, they would leave the state. The public was becoming concerned that they would not have sufficient doctors to tend to their needs.

At 10:00 A.M., the doorbell to the office rang. Sean assumed it was Jennifer or Bertha, arriving a little late. Sean went to the door and saw a beautiful bouquet of fall flowers from a well-known Charles Street florist. The attached card was addressed to Roland. It was not uncommon for Roland to receive flowers from his many female admirers. Sean could not resist reading the card: "Congratulations, Roland, on your remarkable victory in Worcester." The card was signed "Love, Isabella," with a P.S. "You can reach me at my condo after 7:00. How about cocktails and dinner?"

Evidently, Roland and Quigley had already been on the phones bragging to everyone they spoke to about their great victory. They were probably planning a gala celebration party at The 21st, their favorite watering hole, that evening. Sean checked the answering service and, sure enough, there were already twenty calls from Boston cronies, lawyers and judges, federal and state administrators congratulating Roland and Quigley on the medical victory. A Boston Globe reporter had called and wanted to know the details of the case. All callers planned to be at The 21st that evening for the great victory party. The callers mentioned Roland and Quigley by name. One, "Quigley, we knew you could do it. You're the best. Let's tip a few Fosters." Another said, "Rosie, you are the best of the best." Another one, "Rosie, you're a great lawyer. This last victory simply adds more luster to your greatness. Let's have a few for the road." Sean felt an anguished sting so deep he thought he might puke. Not one caller mentioned him by name. He felt so frustrated, so used, so unappreciated, so useless, so unrecognized. No matter what great success he achieved for MM&M, his employers would inevitably claim all the credit. His success would always be their public success, never his own.

This frustration was eating away at him and he was growing more and more angry and resentful. He recalled the early social gatherings and how he was troubled by Roland and Quigley claiming credit for his trial accomplishments. They always described the trial settlement as "our success." Truly it was a success, it was their case that they scooped up or rain-made, but it was not their trial achievement. They did not prepare the case for trial or for settlement. Sean longed for his happier, if less rewarding, days when he tried his own cases, usually small and referred by some distant family member, but cases he could claim as his own.

He was caught in a trap. His unhappiness and dissatisfaction were growing by leaps and bounds. And it was a common financial trap too, the success syndrome, making more money than he could dream of if he were on his own, but being miserable while doing it. He felt he had sold his soul to the devil and could regain his freedom only if he made the final break, regardless of the financial repercussions to himself or his growing family. He knew the financial bubble would burst and he would have no cases or income once he left the 3Ms. He was trapped and he knew it.

Sean glanced at his upcoming trial schedule. With the quick and unexpected settlement of the Worcester case, he had an open three weeks. He decided he could ride the tiger one more time, but the next case he tried for MM&M would be his "sayonara case." It would definitely be his last trial. To try this last case, he would require total control. He knew that if he could control the case and his fee, he would have the financial resources to free himself from the MM&M entanglement. Sean smiled for the first time that morning and he immediately felt contentment and satisfaction at his courage to make this decision. He knew it was the right decision. He would leave MM&M after his next trial.

Sean saw a picture of Rosie and Quigley as they truly were and not as he wished them to be. They were superb at cruising the bar scene and each had their own unique style and charisma. Rosie, in particular, was a piece of work. His wild lifestyle and financial success always amazed Sean. Rosie was fifty-six, totally bald, but had the striking good looks of a Greek god. He looked so much like Yul Brenner that some of his cronies started calling him "Yul." He was a sharply dressed, impressive aging bachelor. He always wore tailor-made Brooks Brothers suits. He had a striking presence and his good looks commanded attention.

Rosie actually considered himself an actor. He did have quite an act. He was a charmer and loved to tell corny jokes. His spiel, not too subtle, was bragging and boasting. Rosie said he never let the facts or reality get in the way of a great story. Unfortunately, his simplistic spiel became a bore the second trip around the club scene because all of his jokes were usually locked on the same channel and he lacked backup material. He was the master of redundancy. However, there was no question that his strikingly, handsome good looks, engaging chatter, and charming demeanor made him a pure entertainer and a bar star. Rosie was the perfect salesman who always knew how to promote himself, and he was always rainmaking the potential referral lawyers at the bar. His lead-ins were simple:, "I just had a major multi-million-dollar trial and made tons of money for Joe Smith. Why not send me some of your PI or medical cases and you'll be in Florida or sailing the Caribbean like Joe?" Little did the impressed listeners know that the case was not settled for a million dollars. It was settled for much less and the real Joe Smith was not sailing the Caribbean but was still working three jobs with a lifetime injury he should have received much more for. The truth be known, Rosie made a quick settlement on this case simply to move it. The client, rather than being the benefactor, was the loser and probably would never sail Boston Harbor, much less the Caribbean, with the pitiful quick settlement he received.

But, Rosie sure could sound impressive and, after one too many scotches all around, his excessively exaggerated war stories gained barroom credibility. His fantasy world became reality. The bar perennials and groupies hung on his every word like they were the proven formula for making a quick buck. Then, invariably, the best Cuban cigars would be distributed to each of his potential referrals. The overhead bar lights gleamed on Rosie's shiny bald head as if he were on a Vaudeville stage as he gleefully handed out elongated Cuban cigar to each of his cronies, "This is to celebrate another big one. Why don't you enjoy a good cigar? Nothing but the best for my friends and referrals. Hi guys. Want another drink? Bartender, another round. Nothing but the best for my friends."

Quigley, on the other hand, was a burnt out fifty-year old and looked all of his years. He actually looked more like a man in his sixties. But how he loved the good life and his "Fosters brews." Quigley was of very tiny physical stature and barely reached the top of the bar. However, he had a very strong athletic figure and his physical presence was very impressive. He wore a striking dark blue patch over his left eye that made him stand out. Big A, as he was affectionately known by his bar cronies, had a very cultured Australian accent and was a great singer of song; he was a born entertainer. On his dark side, Big A had a quick temper and, when he became upset or angry, people genuinely feared for their physical safety as he tended to love to have a good fight. In his other life in Australia, he had been a national golden glove feather weight winner and you never knew if you crossed him the wrong way, when he would resort to become physically intimidating. He was melancholy at times, happy at times, and he had to be watched at all times as his mood was very mercurial. However, to the world generally, Big A was the perfect caricature of the happy, light-hearted, heavy-drinking, smart talking, engaging, comic Australian. Big A longed for world travel and financial freedom but did not have the resources to make that happen. Big A knew all the ins and outs of the Boston political scene, the latest gossip, where the bodies were buried. He knew the leading politicians and the old and new characters on the Boston scene, where they drank, how much, who they dated, their happiness or unhappiness in their marriage, their genealogy, their strengths and foibles. Big A simply knew about everyone, their weakness more than their strengths, their flaws more than their virtues, and he effectively used this arsenal to intimidate. He had the sharpest tongue and you never knew against whom it would be directed. His Australian good looks, personal charm and charisma, story telling ability and love of song made him popular and attractive within bar circles, both drinking and legal. Big A was extremely bright and clever and well read. He could quote at length all the great English and American writers and discuss the latest book on the New York Times best seller list. He hung out with fellow Aussies, Irish immigrants and Harvard cronies in Cambridge and Boston and his close friends were well-known actors, writers, poets, and local politicians and bigwigs. Big A also had a beautiful voice and he would usually be the last to leave the party. He never left without a few Aussie drinking songs. If you didn't know his many angry moods, you would believe he was the perfect Aussie.

Big A had the right political contacts and was famous for his sudden, last minute trips to London. He was rumored to be a literary agent for several well-published English writers and an entertainment agent for a famous Australian rock band. Big A was big and well known socially in the Boston bar scene and was very friendly and well regarded in charitable and religious circles. His name and picture frequently appeared in the social calendar of the Boston Globe. Big A was certainly connected to the right people, he was a true Boston rainmaker – an El Nino – he had all the right political connections, he knew all the right municipal people, he knew how to get things done behind the scenes. Through his broad network of knowing secretaries and receptionists throughout the city and all the Boston law firms, Big A knew the strengths and weaknesses of most of the leading attorneys of the Yankee law firms. He knew which senior attorneys were being pushed into retirement, which law partners were squabbling, which blue blood firm was about to disintegrate, who in the firm had a drinking or drug problem, whose marriage was on the verge of a break-up, which client wore his pants long, which client wore his pants short. To put it simply, he knew all the dirt and used it to his advantage.

Any insight and surveillance always proved invaluable to MM&M when suing doctors and hospitals represented by the elite Boston firms. Big A also knew the friendly and vulnerable insurance adjusters at the insurance companies and knew well the underpaid and under-appreciated claims managers who frequented the bar to complain about their plight in life. Frequently, over a few pints of Fosters or, if the claims adjuster happened to be Irish, Guinness or Murphy's stout, some perfectly timed Aussie drinking songs and poems, Big A would entertain the adjuster at his favorite bar. After a few songs and some great jokes, the adjuster would be interested in settling his automobile rear-ender for big money. Big A's style was to settle at the bar over a few drinks and not at the bar in Court which he considered an expensive and unnecessary delay. Big A liked to move and settle cases and, like Rosie, he believed in quick turn over. Many of his clients received their money quickly. Their cases were never tried and were discounted. Big A, in many ways, was the one who knew all the tricks. He prided himself in not trying cases but in letting others do the difficult trial work. He hated to do the day-to-day **work** on a lawsuit so, if he sent it to you, you knew you would be doing 110% of the work. Big A didn't pretend he wanted to work on the case or prepare the case for trial. If he referred any of his medical cases to Sean, his only promise was that he would use his contacts to try to help resolve the matter. Occasionally, his contacts were helpful but, more than not, they were mere Aussie bar flies and hangers on whose deeds did not measure up to their empty promises. You also had to be very careful when working on one of Big A's medical cases because he made them sound great but, after you learned the medical details and inner workings of the case, the cases were usually disasters and born losers. You could lose your legal reputation on one of his cases overnight.

<u>Chapter 3</u>

Mecca of Medicine

Over the past three years Sean had become very familiar with the flaws and inadequacies of medical care and the errors of the medical profession. He knew about the bad doctors in Massachusetts and the unreliable hospitals and medical clinics. He knew that, to the world, Boston was considered the Mecca of medicine, but in his mind it was also the Mecca of medical neglect, bad medicine, and militant medical societies protecting bad doctors. Through his string of medical cases and years of intense practice, he recognized names and knew background information about the bad doctors in Boston and its suburbs. He knew the hospitals that had used defective incubators, the clinics that had used defective pap smear equipment, and which ones were misdiagnosing cervical cancer. He knew the primary care physicians who didn't perform biopsies or follow-up for breast cancer. He knew the surgeons who neglected to follow the discovery of a lump with an ultrasound test because of cost factors. He was aware of an anesthesiologist in a North Shore hospital who was responsible for three deaths because of failure to properly hydrate a patient before surgery. He knew about emergency room doctors who did not know how to properly examine patients for heart disease. He also was becoming aware of doctors who were operating in community hospitals without training as emergency room doctors and who were not able to diagnose extreme emergency cases. In other words, Sean knew where many of the medical bodies were buried and he knew his list of bad doctors and bad hospitals could go on endlessly. He thought, "If only the general public, the citizens of Massachusetts, could truly see the level of inferior care that their loved ones, relatives and friends were being exposed to in this totally unregulated medical climate." He knew that the medical societies were protecting doctors and the general public could not rely on them to report bad doctors. He also knew that the hospitals protected their staff surgeons and physicians so the public could not rely on them either to expose any wrongdoing. The instinct was to cover up for medical neglect, not to expose it. Medical malpractice litigation had become much more hostile and aggressive, and very stressful over the past few years. Sean believed that successful settlements and trials in medical malpractice cases were one of the only hopes for medical care to improve. The medical societies, hospitals, and surgeons themselves would not, of their own initiative, likely to change and begin to protect the public from bad medicine. Sean was practicing in an area where he no longer was the bull but the bulls eye and because of his aggressive litigation, he was becoming more subject to personal attacks by other law firms, physicians, and hospitals.

It was not happenstance that over the last several months he and his wife had been awakened by mysterious 3:00 A.M. phone calls. This usually happened when he was in the middle of a major medical case and sometimes the phone rang more than three times in a single morning. No one ever replied to his "hello." His solution was to get an unpublished number and that worked for a period of time. But sometimes he still received mysterious early morning calls.

Sean also noticed that more insurance companies were threatening a counter-suit if he sued their physician or their insured. His malpractice insurers were constantly threatening to terminate his liability coverage because he was becoming subject to more claims from frivolous suits. And he was starting to get more complaints filed against him by the Mass. Bar Association that were generated by State Street firms and based on unfounded complaints initiated by their physicians. These complaints were always frivolous and pointless, but they required a great deal of time to rebut. Sean lived in fear that he would have his license taken away because of these frivolous suits. The medical malpractice pot was boiling and anyone suing a doctor or hospital in Massachusetts was a target for intense litigation. The Massachusetts Hospital Association and the medical insurance establishments were major employers in Boston and they were definitely on the offensive and striking back aggressively at plaintiff's lawyers who were foolish enough to take them on.

To add to the mix, medical no-fault insurance bills were pending in the legislature and the media was identifying trial lawyers as barracudas, mercenaries, and money hounds. Lawyer bashing was now an accepted way of life. Often when Sean went out to parties he would be reluctant to identify himself as a lawyer; he didn't want to become the butt of lawyer jokes. Sean also noted that certain of the powerful medical insurers were starting to publish throughout Massachusetts the name, address, and specialty of any doctor who dared to testify in a medical case against any of their insured's. Insurers would then send this information to physicians. This, of course, was a blatant peer pressure tactic used to blackmail, intimidate and deter any doctor who was thinking of testifying against his or her colleagues to testify on behalf of the defense. Some of Sean's most respected experts in well-known specialties and practices were now under tremendous peer pressure and were telling him that they could not testify for the plaintiff, even though the cases did have merit. Sean found that, despite Massachusetts having some of the best medical schools in the world and the best teaching hospitals and doctors, these physicians were no longer ready or willing to cross the line and testify on a medical malpractice case, even when there was obvious negligence or improper care. The potential for reprisals by members of their profession, or their teaching groups, or even their hospitals was just too great. For the first time, the teaching hospitals were defending bad doctors, bad practices, and bad medicine. This tactic, of course, was adversely affecting the quality of medical care. Sean wondered where this misplaced priority would lead. He could see that medical stonewalling would only add fuel to the fire and cause more medical malpractice suits than less. To Sean, who had a strong sense of equity and justice, this seemed totally illogical, bizarre and ridiculous. But, this is what was happening. Sean also noticed this trend among the HMO's in Massachusetts. There were moves to limit their liability to $20,000 rather than holding them completely responsible for negligent acts. Sean saw this as yet another means of adding to the overall problem and ultimately lower standards of medical care.

Sean was beginning to dread the evening's celebration at The 21st because he knew he would have to withstand Rosie and Big A's unending bragging and boasting. He was, however, so exhausted physically and emotionally from the Worcester case that he did look forward to having a drink or two of Guinness to numb his brain and to temporarily forget his foreboding. It might even be fun to hear Big A crack a few good Aussie jokes and sing some good Aussie songs. Big A, when he was on (and he usually was after a few drinks), had great humor and wit. He was blessed with exceptional timing and knew how to entertain an audience with a good story. He had that great combination of humor, warmth, and timing that you can't teach or imitate; you either have it or you don't.

Sean could never match Big A joke for joke. He only knew a few good jokes and didn't have the unique timing or right turns of phrase to make it sound hilariously funny like Big A did. Big A was a born storyteller and comedian, and could improvise with the best of them. He should have been an actor or a stand-up comic rather than a lawyer. Big A's interesting strategy in meeting women was simple. His tactic would be to confront twenty women directly without having met them before, and ask them for an "intimate date." Many of them would refuse the invitation and they often found his conversation and conduct offensive. Some would slap him, others would just walk away, but once in a while one would say yes. Big A said that one for twenty wasn't bad and this line was always a crowd-pleaser. His cronies, however, knew that Big A was all talk and that women were not on the top of his agenda. His life revolved around having a good drink, good bar conversation, socializing and entertaining his cronies. He truly was one of the boys.

The 21st was a gathering place for Boston's newly arriving Irish and Aussie immigrants. So many brogues floated around the bar that it sounded like an actual pub in Sydney, Dublin, Kerry, Donnegal or Cork. Sean, although he didn't like to admit it, often enjoyed and had fun talking with the various writers, poets, actors and hangers-on who patronized The 21st. He found the Irish and Aussies he met to be creative and fun loving and he enjoyed their company. He loved to listen to them discuss "the troubles" and how matters were being resolved. Sean wondered if, now that the Irish were again making their mark and becoming economically successful, they would be tolerant of other emerging minorities like they wished the

Yankee ruling class had been to their ancestors in the previous century. Sean had his doubts.

Before going over to The 21st, Sean took a quick stroll across the Common, and then walked for a while along Newbury Street. He loved these solitary walks. His mind would drift into another world and his anxieties and worries would fade into the distance. He truly loved Boston. He delighted in people-watching and enjoyed the various activities going on: the sidewalk musicians, touch football games on the Common, the array of wandering tourists, smiling mothers with happy, excited children, intrepid squirrels crossing the Commons, beautiful flowers, the fresh air of fall, and the interesting Boston skyline and architecture. Sean meditated in his own world and, for the first time that day, he felt refreshed and content. His life had meaning and purpose.

"Now," he thought, "I'm ready to change my life" and he vowed to have a grand evening at The 21st. His liberation was at hand and he wanted to enjoy it.

Chapter 4

The 21st

The 21st, like most of the trendy Boston watering holes, was crowded with men and women, bumper to bumper, searching for a good time. The drinking crowd was primarily young, twenty and thirty-year-old professionals, both male and female with a steady sprinkling of aging lawyers, stockbrokers, bankers, and financial types. As usual, the bar was humming and always seemed to be at highest pitch from 5:30 to 10:30 P.M. Everyone was frolicking, enjoying conversation and drink, and having that last one "for the road," although it usually did not end in just one drink. At The 21st you could anticipate the unexpected.

This was the night for the victory party and time for Rosie and Quigley to hold court and reign supreme. Sean arrived around 6:30 P.M. and knew that his partners were already there and had enjoyed more than one good Scotch or pint of Fosters. All of The 21st was buzzing about the $2 million settlement, even before Sean arrived. Rosie and Big A never could keep quiet. Sean smiled at how meaningless the confidentiality agreement was and thought, "Why shouldn't the world know that one of the largest hospitals in the state had used defective incubators and was endangering the lives of infants? Isn't the public supposed to know so that these errors and defective machines can be replaced before they burn or kill another baby?" He tried to clear his mind of the incubator case, wanting to have a good time and avoid shoptalk. But each one of Sean's pores was oozing with the law case and, with the crowd buzzing about it, he knew it would be hard not to join in. He ordered a Guinness and soon melted into the surging sea of humanity congregating all around the several small bars.

Suddenly he heard a familiar loud voice, "Sean, come on over. I want you to meet someone." Sean knew he was probably needed as a prop for window dressing. Rosie liked to impress his many lawyer friends, cronies, and potential referrals. So, as Sean slowly made his way over, he wondered what bull Rosie had already slung. He was holding court like a potentate, wound up, full of himself and was ready to let it all hang out. His blue pinstripe suit and red handkerchief shone in the faint neon of the bar, and his white teeth reflected the little visible light. Scotch and water in hand, Rosie smiled and said in a booming voice, "Sean, I want you to meet a great friend of mine! Henry, say hello to Sean. Henry's one of the best and most hard working and underpaid members of the Social Security Board. Henry and I go way back. We both played football for Stonehill College, the Notre Dame of the East, and both were co-captains. Henry sits on my cases and the fact that we know each other doesn't taint your impartiality, does it Henry?" Henry, who seemed a little under the weather, or two sheets to the wind, smiled and said "Of course not, Rosie. Why should I think less of you because we were best friends in college, drinking buddies, and co-captained the best football team Stonehill ever had?"

Rosie laughed. "Henry has his way with words," and went on, "but on a serious note, Henry never shortchanged me on any case I had before him. He has a wonderful sense of justice and, in fact, that justice will probably prevail again when I appear before him Monday. But, Henry, let's not discuss that case yet."

Henry laughed and Sean stood there like a dummy wondering why he had been called over to listen to Rosie's incorrigible boasting and incessant bragging. Sean thought Rosie had not one honest bone in his body. He was the Bill Clinton of his times, so artificial, so insincere, but oh so successful!

Rosie was more than rainmaking. He was the El Nino of boastful words: "Henry, I just won a biggie in Worcester. I spent three years on the case and blew them out of the water. Didn't I, Sean?"

Perhaps it was the Guinness that made him giddy but, Sean, instead of the usual "yes man" response that Rosie expected, said sharply in a loud and angry voice, "I think we **both** spent a lot of time on that case, didn't we, Rosie?" Rosie's smile waned and when he responded, it was in a less loud and more humble voice. Without missing a beat, he said, "Yeah, Henry. Sean and I, we both really worked up that case and we got a great multi-million dollar settlement that no other firm, big or small, could have achieved. Sean, was that $3 or $4 million?" Rosie was already gilding the lily, exaggerating the settlement; two became four and, before the night was over, everyone would be saying the case was settled for $10 million. He knew how to sell himself and the word "I" was never a stranger or orphan in his boasting. He was now unstoppable. "Henry, I think those big over-rated State Street firms are afraid of us. They never try cases. They always settle. What do you think, Henry?" Henry replied, "Rosie, I didn't know you did jury cases. I thought you did state and federal disability work." Rosie said, "With Sean, a proven litigator, we now handle all the big complex medical cases. Henry, if you want to retire to Florida or ever come across a good medical or product case, give me a call. I like to make money for my old classmates."

Sean was trying to nurse his Guinness but now he took a huge swig, almost downing the entire pint in one gulp. He felt nauseous. Rosie kept using the "I" word and talking about how he had prepared the case. This was pure bovine; pure horse shit. Rosie barely put in five hours of work on the incubator case over the last three-year period. And Quigley did **no** work on the case. Sean did it all. Those thousands of hours! It nauseated him to think that no matter how much work he did, how much his trial skills led to the settlement, no matter what he did, he never would be given the credit. And not only that, he would only get five percent of the fee! The remaining ninety-five percent would be divided between his rainmaking associates, with most going to Rosie. Sean found himself muttering, "This is legal slavery," and had difficulty controlling his temper.

He left Rosie's area on the pretense of seeing a law school classmate and headed as far away as he could. Rosie was now on a roll, talking non-stop about the Worcester case and his great multi-million dollar victory. From across the room Sean could see he was schmoozing with the Boston Globe court reporter, whom Sean knew would write about the case. Since he was a crony of Big A's, he would give both he and Rosie name recognition and credit for the case. Sean's name would never be mentioned. Sean muttered to himself, "Perhaps the second Stout is having some effect. What a rip-off artist." He hoped that he said these words to himself and not too loud.

Big A stood at in the far end of the bar regaling his cronies. He stayed clear of Rosie as, instinctively, both rainmakers took different areas, working both ends of the bar. Rosie tended to wander around glad-handing people while Big A liked to lean on the bar, pontificate, and have people come to him. He didn't like to move around much, but his jolly voice and phony laugh could be heard throughout the room. Sean could see that Big A, too, was in good form. After a few pints and several Fosters, Big A was anything but remorseful and melancholy. In fact, he was exuberant. When he drank, he became garrulous and exuded happiness. After drinking, he tended to be very direct and candid whereas Rosie, after drinking, tended to exaggerate and boast. Big A did not speak with a forked tongue, he told it like it was.

Seeing Sean, Big A immediately waved to him and asked him to join the small group of writers, actors, hangers-on, and Boston polls clustered around him. He turned to his compatriots and said, "You see Rosie over there bragging about the case? Well, gentlemen, you see before you Sean, the Babe Ruth of our law office, the true big number three-hitter. It was Sean who hit the home run in Worcester and, if the truth ever be known, which it will not, Rosie and I were there for the ride. Yes, it was our case, but Sean actually did all the preparation over three years and then won the great settlement."

Sean was stunned by Quigley's candidness. He knew that after a few more drinks and a few more stories, these Irish cronies would still believe that Rosie and Quigley won the case, regardless of what Quigley said. Still, Sean beamed for the first time and his smile matched Rosie's. He felt fully content for the first time that evening. Among Quigley's cronies were Cambridge intellectuals who loved to discuss the creative aspects of the trial. They asked Sean a few pertinent questions about the case and then continued to enjoy Quigley. Quigley, himself, was truly impressed with the amount of the settlement. He was not a malpractice attorney. His specialty was more in the corporate area and he did not really know how to try a complex medical case. The fact that he and his friends seemed truly impressed with Sean's accomplishment gave Sean a great sense of satisfaction.

As he stood by, Quigley casually tapped him on the shoulder and said, "Sean, I want to talk to you about one of my cases. Do you have a few minutes?" Sean replied, "Big A, what is it? Anything wrong?" He always feared the worse because Quigley was never serious unless he was in trouble or had some financial crisis. "Sean, you won't believe it, but I am handling this great kidney case sent to me by one of my corporate friends. It involves a thirteen-year-old girl who was misdiagnosed for six years by her doctors and is now at risk of dying because of two badly infected and broken down kidneys. She is desperate for a transplant and may die soon. It's my best case and I know I should have referred it to you sooner but, I thought with a few calls to the friendly adjuster, I could settle it. I was wrong and now I'm in real trouble. The case is scheduled for trial in a few weeks, but it isn't ready. It needs a ton of work. I was hoping you would work the case up and try it. I know it's totally over my head. I know you can somehow prove the doctors misdiagnosed this girl's condition. Can you help me?"

Sean replied, "I'm exhausted from trying too many of Rosie's medical cases. Eight trials in eight months is too much. Now Rosie has handed me some more cases and the case load is too much for any one lawyer to handle. I feel like I'm totally overwhelmed. If I take your kidney case, Big A, it will be a miracle for any lawyer, no matter how skilled and ambitious, to get that case ready in a few weeks. It just can't be done; it's a lot to ask of me, to undertake the burden of this case when I'm totally exhausted from this horrific trial schedule." Quigley sat silently, looking disappointed. Sean's mind was clicking quickly, however. Was it the Guinness? Was this kidney case his passport to release from his servitude at MM&M? Suddenly, and without much thought, Sean said, "If I take this case and prepare it for trial and try it, I want to have total control. I also want to share sixty percent of the contingent fee. I want total authority to make all settlement and trial decisions and total control over the entire case from trial to verdict. I don't want you to have any authority to settle this case and I alone dictate whether to settle or go to jury verdict. I don't want you to settle this kidney case," he went on "like Rosie did in the incubator case, after I've put in three long tough years of tedious detailed work. I don't intend to settle this kidney case, but to go to jury verdict. I will prepare a written agreement as to what my legal fee will be. Tomorrow, sign it and put it on my desk with your entire file. Are these terms acceptable to you?"

Sean knew unless the agreement was in writing he couldn't trust Quigley, nor for that matter **any** attorney, to honor an oral agreement. He had been burned in the past by referring attorneys who did not honor their oral promises and he vowed it would never happen again. While Quigley considered the terms, Sean thought about how business was conducted these days. Even with his close associates, everything had to be detailed in writing. Trust was a fragile commodity in MM&M and anything relating to money had to be in writing. Most referral attorneys were known for being tough business lawyers. They would fight the trial lawyer who won the case for them for any portion of his fee, and, if the case was lost, they would try to have the trial attorney pick up all the expenses. Life was cruel and tough for the civil litigator. You had to keep your head up at all times. Otherwise, you could come out on the short end of the stick. This said volumes as to why trial lawyers were insecure and had phobias about trusting people and why they died young.

Sean was amazed at his own boldness. He was talking as if he were in control, and he sounded very businesslike. He thought that it must be the Guinnesses speaking, giving him unusual calmness and fortitude. But Sean thought he saw a light at the end of the tunnel with this kidney case. He saw the case freeing him from the financial shackles at MM&M and giving him the liberty to be on his own and independent. The kidney case suddenly had become the most important one of his life. Quigley did not attempt to negotiate with Sean to cut his share of the fee.

Sean assured Quigley that he would do the best he could to prepare the kidney case for trial. Quigley, in turn, muttered that he knew some doctors newly arrived to the Boston area that could be helpful at the last minute. But Sean knew that Quigley was a great talker who sounded good at the bar but rarely delivered when necessary. If he had the medical experts ready on hand, wondered Sean, why did he wait two weeks prior to trial to refer the case? He had learned never to trust Quigley or Rosie as they promised the stars but seldom, if ever, delivered the goods. Their word was as good as a cloud of smoke.

But, this time Sean was content to have a case that he believed would launch his new independent career. He ordered another Guinness, his third. He didn't seem to care. He enjoyed the rest of the evening, listening to the immigrants talking about the old sod, the many beautiful lassies they had left behind, their wonderful Irish experiences, and how peace can finally be restored to Ireland.

When Sean woke up at home the next morning, he had some serious explaining to do. His wife, Miriam, immediately confronted him about the unopened luggage still standing in the dining room. It was a puzzle to Sean too and he tried to explain how his social obligations caused him to party all night, which didn't really sit too well with Miriam. Sean believed in being direct and honest, even if his excuse involved getting caught up in conversations with beautiful stewardesses. Sometimes, the truth hurt Miriam momentarily, but she knew from the details of Sean's explanation, and the party-boy reputation of Quigley and Rosie, that her husband was a fish out of water and was very likely an innocent bystander. Sean explained to her that he had made a big decision. He would try one last case and then leave MM&M. If he could win this last case, he would have control of sixty percent of the fee and, for the first time, they would have some financial independence. Miriam's initial anger at him had cooled and she now seemed relieved that Sean was leaving the firm. She knew he had not been happy, especially over the last year, he had talked constantly of his discontent and had even considered leaving the profession. Miriam seemed happy with his decision. They shared a lovely morning drinking coffee and looking forward to a happier future. Even with a hangover, Sean seemed relieved that he had finally made the decision.

Chapter 5

The Kidney Case

The next day Sean didn't get to the office until 11:30 A.M. He felt lighthearted and couldn't wait to start on the new case. To his surprise, on top of his desk was a detailed note from Quigley and, in his unique Palmer method of writing, it set forth, in detail, the terms and conditions Sean had proposed at The 21st Bar. The note was brief and to the point:

> This kidney case is yours to prepare and try. Your fee is sixty percent of the forty percent contingent fee. You and you alone have full authority to control, dismiss, settle, or to go to ultimate verdict with this case. Just keep me advised of all developments. Call me any time if I can help. But, as this case needs a lot of detail work, I leave the total responsibility of preparation to you. The defendants are represented by attorney Chauncy Howe at Howe & Gates. His firm represents forty percent of the teaching hospitals and doctors in Boston and also the Massachusetts Medical Society.

They play rough and will paperwork
you to death. Howe cannot be
trusted – his tactic is to threaten
opposing lawyers with malpractice
and report them to the BBO for
disbarment. Howe & Gates are
politically well connected and are
very friendly with Judge Taylor, the
judge assigned to Lisa's case. Watch
out for Taylor as he never met a
plaintiff's lawyer he liked. He is
very pro-defendant and is not known
for being impartial. Taylor will do
anything to deep six the case. No
plaintiff's attorney has ever won a
medical case before him. Talk to me
if you need any help. I can be
reached at the Barrister Hotel in
London. Bertha has my number.
Good luck! Big A.

Quigley's note jolted Sean back to reality.
He knew his chance of winning the case was a long
shot, but his chance of receiving any fee was now
non-existent. He never should have said he would
take the case. What a fool he was! Quigley had
waited until he was relaxed after a few pints of
Guinness and then dumped the kidney case on him.
Then he took off to England. Sean muttered, "God,

that Guinness stuff is truly the curse of the Irish. They would have ruled the world if it weren't for that stout." Sean realized that now he would be butting heads with one of the most feared and respected State Street firms in Massachusetts – confronting the blue blood establishment head on. Howe & Gates was the best medical defense firm in the city. They had never lost, or even settled, a malpractice case. Their senior trial attorneys held influential positions on the Massachusetts Bar Judicial Nominating Committee and on the Board of Bar Overseers and they had a tremendous network of political and judicial connections. Howe & Gates had disbarred many a plaintiff's malpractice attorney; they played the game rough.

Attorney Howe's reputation for being feared in the courtroom was well-earned. He was the dean of the defense bar and, at age fifty-five, was on top of his game. He bragged to opposing plaintiff's counsel that he never lost a case. Howe was intimidating, and he knew how to generate bushels of troublesome paperwork and legal briefs, which wore down many a plaintiff's attorney so that very few cases could even reach the jury for verdict. He was a master at dismissing cases on technical grounds and he usually had friendly judicially connected trial judges ruling in his favor. The medical and legal establishment worked together in strange ways. Howe & Gates literally hated plaintiffs' medical lawyers. This elite firm zealously and effectively represented the powerful lobbying efforts of the Massachusetts Medical Society to pass a no-fault medical bill favorable to the medical profession. All Howe & Gates attorneys had some Ivy League background, the majority from Harvard and Yale. They graduated at the top of their class, and wore their school colors, their bow ties, their multi-colored suspenders, and pin striped suits with great pride and relish. Howe & Gates represented the cream of the medical and corporate establishment. Their list of clients was like reading the Dow Jones Index firms representing the best corporations not just of the state or nation, but world-wide.

Sean dejectedly sat in his office, shocked and overwhelmed. His so-called "last case" already looked hopeless. All the odds were against him. He was still exhausted from working so hard over the past eight months. Now, instead of a break, he had to try a complex malpractice case against the best defense team in Boston and it all had to be handled in a short three weeks. He scanned the skimpy file. Outside of the Contingent Fee Agreement and executed medical releases, it was paper thin. It was hard to believe that this case was three weeks from trial and didn't even contain any medical records! He saw the Pro Se Complaint, which Quigley had never amended. This was sloppy and, at trial, could present problems. He noted that the case was filed in court only one day before it would have been dismissed because of the three-year statute of limitations. Luckily, Quigley was saved by his client's Pro Se filing the case. Otherwise he would have been sued for malpractice for blowing the statute of limitations.

Scan noted that the answers to the defendant's interrogatories were inadequate, almost non-responsive. Quigley had never actually met with the client to go over the questions, but had worked up the first draft on his own. This was the quick way, but was slapdash and very dangerous because it could lead to incomplete and inaccurate answers. The client could then be impeached and devastated at trial and would look ridiculous on the stand. These "no brainer" answers would definitely have to be supplemented and answered correctly to save the client from being seriously destroyed on cross-examination.

It was a miracle that Attorney Howe had not filed a Motion to Dismiss, as it was obvious that the plaintiff's case was not properly prepared. Howe's failure to act led Sean to believe that he hoped the plaintiff's attorney would not wake up until it was too late. Judge Taylor would be happy to entertain a Motion to Dismiss on legal technicalities. Howe planned not to launch the fatal blow until the time of trial. Then he would strike with the Motion to Dismiss. He was sneaky and smart, and his defense tactics were ingenious. Howe figured he would strike at the jugular and win the case before one witness even testified. The result? The plaintiff would be deprived of a jury trial. Defendant wins. Plaintiff loses.

Howe played the paper game like a master chessman and was so far ahead that the plaintiff was already on the verge of defeat. The Pre-trial conference was scheduled for the next afternoon and tomorrow. Sean feared the worse. He knew he was in an almost hopeless position. Many attorneys who were less seasoned and determined would be trying to save face in this situation and would quietly, and voluntarily, dismiss the case. But Sean was not known as a quitter and, despite the odds, he would try to give his new client, Lisa Rowe, her day in court. She, at least, deserved a jury to decide her fate.

Sean was furious with Quigley for the problems he had created. He wondered again how he ever became associated with the likes of Rosie and Quigley. He angrily burst into Quigley's office, ready to challenge him and tell him how Lisa's chance of winning the case was zero. Luckily,

Quigley was not there, and then Sean remembered the note, and Quigley's quick, fun trip to London. He learned from Bertha that Quigley had left a message on her desk too that he was making a "family pilgrimage" to England and Scotland and would be gone for two to three weeks. He said he was visiting Aussie relatives in London, but Sean knew he was taking a "bartender's holiday" and would be maitre d' and bartender at his time-share hotel in London, which he owned with several Boston cronies who had invested in his English home away from home. Quigley always traveled rent-free in London and was treated at his hotel like a US celebrity.

Sean realized that after Quigley wrote the referral note, he had left the scene of the crime and had little interest in helping with the case. For all intents and purposes, Sean was left holding the bag, with the case totally unprepared and unready to go to trial. Sean swore and cursed Quigley: "What a shithead, what a jerk. Doesn't he have a conscience?" But, despite the overwhelming odds and the hopelessness of the situation, Sean vowed he wouldn't quit. "Success is only failure turned inside out," he whispered to himself, "Lisa needs an advocate. She needs someone to help her now, or her case is lost." Sean, too, realized that her situation was becoming more and more desperate by the moment, and more hopeless by the second.

The Pre-Trial conference was scheduled for 10:00 A.M. before Judge Taylor, who was well-known and feared by every plaintiff's attorney. He was pro-defendant and had a definite bias and deep-rooted prejudice against any plaintiff's attorney who brought a medical case into his courtroom. It was rumored that at a recent trial seminar Judge Taylor had said, "When will personal injury attorneys stop flooding the court with worthless and frivolous malpractice cases?"

The Taylor family was prominent in Boston, with family members influential in banking, investment, academic, legal, and medical circles. Judge Taylor, as were most of his family and ancestors, had been educated at Oxford. Many Taylors had graduated from the best Ivy League law schools, which they had endowed with multimillion-dollar trusts. Judge Taylor had spent his first ten years as a defense lawyer in one of the prominent State Street firms and later was appointed by the Republican governor to serve as a Superior Court judge. Now sixty-nine, Taylor was a year from mandatory retirement. He was known for his mean, often outrageous, temper and his short attention span. Always abrupt with the plaintiff's attorneys, their clients and court personnel, he was a fanatic for time scheduling and raced to have his cases tried quickly. The case had to start precisely at 9:00 A.M. He never allowed a witness to be on the stand very long. Even if an examination by the plaintiff was extended, Judge Taylor would interrupt: "Counsel, you're being irrelevant. If you have a point, get to it and let's not bore the jury." Lawyers described him as a terror and a complete embarrassment and he was universally disliked by court personnel and clerks. He was curt with everyone except his cronies and former corporate colleagues from the big name Yankee firms.

Judge Taylor wore a constant frown, had a white unruly mane, blue blood-shot squinty eyes, and florid complexion that turned tomato red when he was at the apex of his anger. He sat on the bench, bent over, his head down, appearing in a contorted position like a lion ready to spring at his prey. An attorney whose mother had died while he was in the middle of a complex medical case had to hand the case over to a first-year, inexperienced trial attorney because Judge Taylor would not delay the case a day so the attorney could attend the funeral. The poor fellow lost his mother and a major case in the same week.

Judge Taylor was known in plaintiff's circles as a bastard who knew how to deep six and destroy cases. He often seemed to act as second defense team for the medical doctor on trial. He usually sustained all the defense objections but rarely, if ever, ruled in favor of the plaintiff's attorney. He loved to interrupt and lecture plaintiff's counsel and cause disruption. Some speculated that he was prejudiced against the plaintiff in medical cases because his brother, Simon, was president of the Massachusetts Medical Society, which lobbied viciously for passage of a medical no-fault bill. His other brother, Josiah, was a prominent podiatrist. His nephew was chief of surgery at the Massachusetts General Hospital. The only time Judge Taylor showed any warmth was when he, with a wide smile, thanked the jury for returning a defendant's verdict in favor of a physician or hospital. Whenever he looked at the jury verdict slip and smiled before stating the verdict, everyone in the courtroom knew it was in favor of the defense.

Sean now had to go before one of the most pro-defendant and unfriendly judges in the state. No medical malpractice case had ever resulted in a plaintiff's verdict when tried in front of Judge Taylor, and the record had held true over the thirty-seven years that he had been sitting on the bench. In addition, Attorney Howe had never lost a medical malpractice case in over thirty years of trial work defending physicians and hospitals. Sean knew that the odds of winning this case were next to zero, but he would not let himself give up.

Sean realized that, even though he was new on the case, he dared not request a continuance from Judge Taylor. That would be a red flag and an obvious tip-off that he was not prepared. He also knew that if he did ask for a continuance, it wouldn't likely be granted anyway, and that the Motion would be vigorously and successfully opposed by Chauncy Howe, who would never give an experienced attorney like Sean any precious time to prepare his case.

Sean was behind the eight ball. He had had only one run-in with Chauncy Howe in the past and it put him near the top of Howe's hate list. Sean had won a six-figure verdict against a radiological clinic in Brookline, which ultimately resulted in the clinic being closed down for using faulty PAP smear equipment. Attorney Howe did not represent the clinic at trial but, after trial, petitioned to have the clinic's license restored. The Department of Public Health denied his request after Sean and his client, along with several hundred women, marched on the State House and vigorously protested the petition. Many misdiagnosed cases of cervical cancer had been caused by the clinical error and after a hotly contested legislative hearing, the clinic was ultimately denied the license. In the process,

Howe and Gates lost one of their well-heeled clients, along with legal fees estimated at several million dollars.

They say "revenge is sweet" and Attorney Howe would soon discover that he now had an opportunity to settle the score and humiliate Sean as much as possible in the process. Trial stakes would get higher by the minute because neither the plaintiff nor the defense counsel liked or respected one another. If the truth be said, the animosity went very deep. A collision of two different cultures now loomed on the horizon – the inner city lawyer versus the established State Street firm. Chauncy Howe and corporate attorneys like him had no love or respect for personal injury attorneys. They called lawyers like Sean ambulance chasers and bottom feeders. On many occasions Howe had said at legal seminars that the sharp increase in medical costs could be directly attributed to exorbitant insurance premiums paid by hospitals and doctors to defend against frivolous suits brought by money-hungry PI attorneys and their fortune-hunting clients.

Only one week before, Chauncy Howe had spoken on behalf of the Massachusetts Medical Society before a legislative hearing in respect to the recent no-fault bill. He was quoted in the Boston Globe saying, "Doctors are highly trained specialists, scientists if you will, and should not be held accountable for their inadvertent errors in medical judgment. If doctors err, they err trying to help the patient and, if anyone shall bear the cost, it is best for the economy that the patient bears such cost for the injury and not the medical profession.

Sean gagged when he read this. "The world is upside down," he thought. "Doctors are above the law and not accountable, even if their misdeeds kill the patient." This was hogwash.

To Sean, Chauncy Howe was the epitome of everything he disliked about the legal defense bar and the pompous and arrogant medical establishment. He believed that medical responsibility and accountability were critical to the promotion of quality of care in Massachusetts and around the country. Doctors and hospitals were not above the law, nor should anyone be. To Sean, accountability and responsibility enhanced rather than eroded the quality of medical care. He believed that consumers and medical services were entitled to have cases performed in accordance with the accepted standards, and that doctors and hospitals should not be rewarded and encouraged when they didn't meet that standard but should be held accountable for their mistakes. No one, not even a highly paid or highly skilled physician or medical practice, should be above the law.

Chapter 6

Against All Odds

As an experienced trial lawyer, Sean had first-hand knowledge that the medical establishment and insurance companies would respond to changes only when their errors were exposed, especially after a six or seven figure verdict for the other side. These powerful industries were not proactive but reactive. They responded to large financial penalties, but then used these to frighten the public: "These SUITS are out of control and are affecting your insurance premiums." Of course, this was greatly overstated. In the United States, the frequency of six-figure verdicts and multi-million dollar verdicts is very rare and this was a scare tactic used to lobby legislatures and to force passage of restrictive malpractice legislation which would either cap insurance verdicts or limit a plaintiff's recovery to economic losses.

Sean recalled the favorable repercussions within medical circles and the changes that occurred after several of his breast cancer cases. He was able to prove that the treating gynecologists had committed malpractice by not biopsying a long-standing breast lump. These misdiagnoses, which often resulted in the death of a young or middle-age woman, were reported extensively in an expose` by the Boston Globe when the paper spotlighted several of Sean's cases. Ultimately this led to incisive and detailed articles published in the New England Journal of Medicine, which argued for a new standard of care that gynecologists should routinely biopsy and perform ultrasounds on persistent breast lumps.

Sean remembered this with pride, but he regretted that so many women had to suffer and die needlessly before the medical establishment finally blew the horn and started to publicize the need to biopsy early. He thought of the many other cancer cases he had successfully tried involving misdiagnoses of colon, lung, cervical, and prostate cancer and how pleased he had been when these cases were highlighted in newspaper articles and medical journals. Sean knew that when the medical profession was embarrassed or exposed, they would be more likely to change their ways. He regretted that it took them so long to change and that they spent so much time and money defending bad medicine at the expense of the good. The consumer paid the bill and Sean believed that consumers deserved high quality medical care. Medical and insurance resources should not be expended needlessly in defending bad medicine and in protecting bad doctors.

Now he had the burden to prepare an important case for trial and he had to be ready for tomorrow's pre-trial conference. Sean decided not to telephone Chauncy Howe. From a strategic point, he did not want to give him the opportunity to gain the offensive. This, of course, was a little pre-trial gamesmanship, but Sean knew how to play this game and could play it as well as Chauncy Howe any day.

Sean looked down at the records his secretary had just brought in from the pediatric hospital. The records were complete and detailed but they only covered events after the six-year period, when Lisa was finally diagnosed as having two badly damaged kidneys. The most important and significant medical records, however, those covering the critical period during which she was treated by Dr. Smith, the pediatrician, and Dr. Blade and Savin Medical, were not in the file. In other words, Sean was faced with a six-year gap in medical records and it was this gap that he hoped to use to prove that Drs. Smith, Blade, and Savin Medical were negligent in their care of Lisa. Now he faced the nightmare of having no records to study or to show to his medical experts who were supposed to review how the alleged misdiagnosis had occurred. These records were probably in the office files of Drs. Smith, Blade, and Savin

Medical. They would document the diagnostic studies performed, and the results of all tests including urine tests and blood studies. Sean knew that with these records missing, his ability to try the case was seriously hampered. He couldn't possibly learn the facts about the misdiagnosis without them.

He started to panic; he felt lost at sea without a compass. How could he explain the basis and heart of his medical case to Judge Taylor at the pre-trial conference? How could he prove that he had the ability and evidence to establish a prima facie case against the medical providers? Sean's heart was racing and his palms and face were sweaty. He felt like he was about to faint. The more he studied the case, the more hopeless it became – and the closer the trial date loomed.

In the past, Sean had been able to bluff and finesse his way through certain difficult cases. But his success in those cases was due to the fact that he had been opposed by less experienced attorneys and tried by judges who were more friendly to the plaintiff. Sean knew he could not bluff or outwit an experienced attorney like Chauncy Howe. And Judge Taylor was not your everyday friendly trial judge. Taylor gleefully devoured attorneys who were unprepared, especially the plaintiff's attorneys. Sean also knew that Judge Taylor would love to dismiss this case without ever having a witness called. He did not want to be humiliated like that.

He was aware of the importance of the patient's medical records and how effectively they could be used to prove negligence. Documentation details the treatment and provides the heart and soul of a medical case and that's why preserving medical records is critical. Many times Sean had won significant medical malpractice verdicts and settlements because he was able to use entries in the medical record as a weapon against the carelessness of hospital personnel. Medical records could also be used as a sword against negligent doctors. They detailed the thought process and what was, or was not, done for the patient at critical times, which could result in either serious injury or death. Sean recalled one significant case involving an operative death. In that case, he used the hospital records as a means to show that, for the critical seventy-two hours after surgery, the attending surgeon never physically saw the patient or ordered antibiotics to arrest an out-of-control septic infection. This eventually caused the death of a thirty-five-year-old mother. The medical record clearly showed that during this critical period of time, the physician, despite nurses' notes indicating rising fever and patient deterioration, never actually saw the patient.

This made a deep and meaningful impression on the jury and resulted in a substantial verdict.

Sean was now faced with a dilemma. How could he expect to successfully cross-examine Dr. Smith about his substandard care during this six-year period without the medical records and the necessary diagnostic studies? Sean imagined how Louis XVI must have felt right before the guillotine dropped and chopped off his head. He could visualize Judge Taylor and Chauncy Howe pulling the lever. His head would roll because he wasn't prepared.

Sean figured it would take a miracle to save this case from dismissal. Murphy's Law was in control; anything that could go wrong would go wrong. Murphy must have been an Irish lawyer trying a medical malpractice case as hopelessly prepared as this one. Sean agonized again over why he ever accepted the case from Quigley.

As he sat in his office in a daze, trying to think of a way he could wave the white flag, Jennifer burst in and announced that Mr. and Mrs. Rowe and their daughter, Lisa, had arrived for their 3:00 P.M. meeting. Sean was dreading this. Should he tell his clients that it was impossible to try the case because it wasn't prepared? Should he suggest that it might be best to voluntarily dismiss the case before Chauncy Howe assessed attorney's fees and costs against him and against Mr. and Mrs. Rowe? Should he tell them that, based on his review so far and the status of the file, his chance of winning the case was non-existent? No. He couldn't do that. Despite these negative thoughts and the truth, which he knew should be revealed to the Rowes, Sean believed, deep in his heart, that Lisa, the innocent victim of a six-year history of misdiagnosis, deserved to have her day in court. She deserved to win or lose her case before a jury, despite all of the legal obstacles.

Scan was a trained advocate and an experienced medical lawyer and it was his obligation to give Lisa her due. He knew as a trial advocate that Lisa's case must be heard in court and go to a jury verdict, so he vowed right then that he would never surrender hope and request a dismissal of the case. Lisa deserved nothing but his best and most dedicated effort, regardless of how poorly the case had been prepared to date. Sean vowed to himself that he would do everything to win this case and he would go down fighting for his client. That's what a trial lawyer was and why advocating was so important. He would take the case regardless of the odds. He must try the case in court, fight for his client, and go to verdict.

Sean decided to meet the Rowe family in his disorganized office rather than in Rosie's elaborate,

ornate museum of a conference room. He thought
his office was cozier and gave him more privacy,
and it gave his clients a sense of the courtroom.
The office was usually strewn with files and
reminded Sean of the broken-down courtroom
where he tried his cases. A fiftyish looking couple
filed in, followed by a lovely petite young girl with
long black hair and dark brown eyes. Lisa, despite
her fragile appearance, radiated beauty. She looked
much younger than thirteen. Sean realized
immediately that her youthful appearance and
stunted growth must be caused by her kidney
condition. She looked more like a seven-year-old
child. He smiled warmly at Lisa and she responded
with an endearing childish smile when her friendly
brown eyes met his. It was love at first sight. Sean
knew that this case, come hell or high water, would
go to trial and to jury verdict. He was determined
,from the first time he laid eyes upon Lisa, to make
certain that she had her day in court.

  Despite every effort, Sean could not help but
stare at Lisa's arms, both of which were covered
with black and blue marks. They were extremely
thin and bruised from the I.V. needles and dialysis
treatments that Lisa had endured over the last
several years. Sean noted in particular a terrible
disfiguring scar and an opening on her left wrist.
He knew that this was where a permanent shunt was

placed, in order to give her dialysis treatments at the clinic three times a week.

When he spoke to his clients, Sean usually tried to be low key and very casual in order to impart an air of confidence and control. He observed that Lisa was very interested and intrigued by the Indian statue and the wood carving over his desk. Sean interpreted this as a sign that he and Lisa had similar tastes and that Lisa, like him, was an underdog who understood the odds and knew how difficult her case would be. He desperately wanted to be very casual and cool, and not to show his troubled spirit and fears for the future.

Mr. and Mrs. Rowe, by their blanched and tired faces, betrayed their great anxiety and the constant wear and fatigue they had undergone caring for Lisa over the last nine years. Mrs. Rowe, when she talked, spoke very quickly. She was an extremely nervous woman and you could tell she was apprehensive and feared for Lisa's future. Tears always seemed to be welling up in her eyes.

Mr. Rowe barely looked at his wife. He never smiled. He was very reticent, showed very little emotion, and seemed distant. He immediately unnerved Sean with his coldness and detachment and Sean thought neither of the parents would make a very good witness at trial. From only a brief conversation with the parents, Sean could tell that they were on a perpetual guilt trip. They blamed themselves for Lisa's lost kidneys and for the many years wasted with misdiagnosis and neglect by her treating physicians. In almost all medical cases the victim or the parents blamed themselves when something went wrong over a long period of time. Psychologically Sean knew it was important to assure the Rowes that they were not at fault and that Dr. Smith, Dr. Blade, and Savin Medical were responsible for not properly diagnosing Lisa's kidney condition. They were the sole reason Lisa was on dialysis three times a week and had a grave prognosis for the future. She could easily die from her severe kidney infection. Sean realized that his pep talk and his effort to assuage their guilt was not succeeding, but he knew it never would succeed. They had undergone too many years of suffering. The Rowes would always blame themselves and nothing Sean or anyone else could do would change that guilty feeling.

Sean was enraptured by Lisa's angelic face. He was extremely impressed with her. She had such a sweet innocence about her and she seemed to have magical dancing eyes. They immediately caught your attention. She was so radiant, sweet, and precious that one's heart immediately went out to her. You could see by her stunted growth and the telltale marks on her arms that she had suffered terribly over the last few years and had undergone great pain. She had the eyes, look, and complexion of a person that had suffered a great deal in her brief lifetime. However, when she smiled, it lit up the room.

Sean could not help but admire her fortitude, courage, and dignity. He felt if she could testify in court, she would make a tremendous witness because she had the innocence of a child but would be a witness the jury would not be able to look away from. Sean knew that Lisa's prognosis and future were extremely bleak and that she would probably be wedded to a kidney machine for the rest of her life. And every time she went for her dialysis treatments, she suffered the terrible and well-known risk of infection. Frequently, patients die not from the kidney breaking down but from the infection incurred during dialysis. Sean was upset and on the verge of tears when he thought about Lisa's future.

His approach was to be candid with the Rowes and to tell them immediately that he had had a problem obtaining the early medical records. He said he had excellent and very detailed records from Pediatric Hospital and that should be very helpful in the case. He always tried to emphasize the positive to the clients rather to overwhelm them with negative information. They had usually suffered greatly already and were too psychologically compromised to endure any more setbacks.

Mr. and Mrs. Rowe told Sean how much they admired and respected Quigley: what a wonderful person he was; what a great sense of humor he had; how they always received a St. Patrick's Day card from him; how friendly and fun-loving he was when they would occasionally see him at a Red Sox game or other social event. They told Sean how he always assured them that the case was moving along nicely and he was on top of the situation and that everything was being done that could be done. But Sean knew that Quigley had not been candid with the Rowes. He was quick to note that none of the Rowe's comments related to anything Quigley did to prepare or work up the case for trial, only what a great personality he was.

The file before Sean was paper-thin. It contained only a couple of letters from the Rowes, a Contingent Fee Agreement, a few medical authorizations, a few status letters to the Rowes, and an amateurish set of incomplete Answers to Interrogatories. The case was not even close to being ready for trial. The Pediatric Hospital records that Sean had ordered clearly showed the major destruction to both of Lisa's kidneys and the guarded, gray prognosis for the future. The kidney tests were all positive for total kidney failure of one kidney, which meant it was completely damaged, and ninety percent failure of the other. Lisa needed a transplant soon or she was doomed to die very young.

The records showed that if Lisa stopped responding to dialysis, she might die if she did not undergo a successful transplant within six months. To date, the search was still on for a compatible donor and the notes in the file indicated that her treating doctors were concerned whether Lisa would be alive in six months if she did not get a transplant. Her prognosis was now as grave as it possibly could be. Sean did not wish to discuss Lisa's condition in front of her, so when the time came, he asked her to accompany Jennifer on a tour of Rosie's ornate conference room and to look at the lovely view of the Burial Grounds and the Boston Common. He didn't want Lisa to become sad or demoralized hearing any talk about the seriousness of her condition. He felt very protective of his new client.

After Lisa left the room, Mrs. Rowe described in detail how she had cared diligently for her daughter during the early years of her illness. She had faithfully brought Lisa to Dr. Smith and Dr. Blade at the Savin Medical Clinic for all her medical evaluations. Mrs. Rowe said that from age 5 to age 11, Lisa was always sick, always seemed to come down with a virus, and how five or six times a year, when she was seen at Savin Medical, she was usually very sick. She told Sean how supportive the doctors were and how she trusted them both. They had taken care of the Rowe's other two children and were responsive to her telephone calls and always willing to see her. She said she had nothing but confidence and trust in Dr. Smith and Dr. Blade, and was stunned when she learned that for six years they had constantly misdiagnosed Lisa's life-threatening condition.

Mrs. Rowe blurted out, "I'm very angry with Dr. Smith, Dr. Blade, and Savin Medical. I never knew they didn't properly test or treat my daughter. They should have referred her to Pediatric Hospital within the first year and not waited until six years later." She cried as she spoke about how she and her husband were deceived and misled by the doctors' constant reassurances that Lisa was doing well when, in reality, her condition was worsening. She related in detail how her pediatricians, Dr. Smith and Dr. Blade, repeatedly told her that it was not necessary to send Lisa to a Boston hospital because all that the big city hospitals and high priced Boston doctors would do would be to run up the medical bill with unnecessary tests and cause Lisa unnecessary pain.

Every time Mrs. Rowe or her husband asked for another consult or second opinion, Dr. Smith said he would consult with his partner, Dr. Blade. And, of course, Dr. Blade always agreed with Smith's diagnosis. Two or three times a year they would have kidney tests done that involved dip stick studies and urine tests. These were done at Savin Medical, their jointly owned clinic. Mrs. Rowe said that she was told that the urine and blood studies were always negative. Dr. Smith had said that if the tests were positive, he would have referred Lisa to a nephrologist or to Pediatric Hospital for a consult.

She went on to explain that Lisa's symptoms of excessive urine, thirst, and virus conditions would last seven to ten days and then subside and she would be well for three or four weeks, only to have the same symptoms repeat. This went on for approximately six years. It seemed that, after she saw Dr. Smith or Dr. Blade, a few days later, Lisa always seemed to be better. Because Lisa always seemed to get better after these visits, Mr. and Mrs. Rowe assumed that the two doctors had the case well under control and were doing everything possible to treat their daughter. Smith and Blade continually said that Lisa was merely going through normal childhood illnesses and, as she got older, she would grow out of them and the viruses would clear up.

Mrs. Rowe said it was only by chance that Lisa was ever referred to Pediatric Hospital. Drs.

Smith and Blade were on a legal medical seminar in the Caribbean for two weeks when Lisa became violently ill. Because both of her treating doctors were out of town, Mrs. Rowe took Lisa to Pediatric Hospital based on the recommendation of Ms. Paula Murray, Lisa's fourth grade teacher. At Pediatric Hospital, Dr. Grouper and Dr. Hamilton, both board certified nephrologists, ran some basic tests. The very first test on the very first day indicated that Lisa had completely lost one kidney, and the other was ninety percent damaged due to kidney backup.

It was only then that Mr. and Mrs. Rowe learned that both of Lisa's kidneys were permanently damaged, and that this was the result of a six-year chronic infection which was never properly diagnosed. Both nephrologists explained how excessive urine, thirst, and constant viruses were tell-tale signs and a classic indication of kidney infection. They explained how the urine would back up by reflux into the kidney because of the deficit in the ureter, thereby causing the kidney to be continually infected and damaged. Mr. and Mrs. Rowe concluded that if it were not for the good fortune of Ms. Murray's note indicating that Lisa should be referred to Pediatric Hospital, she never would have been diagnosed in time.

After the tests confirmed that Lisa's kidneys were severely damaged, Dr. Smith and Dr. Blade continued to assure Mr. and Mrs. Rowe that they had done everything they could. They claimed to be at a loss to explain how Lisa's kidneys had deteriorated so badly when all the lab and urine studies at Savin Medical, over the six-year period, were negative. They claimed to have done everything according to the book and said that they would not have changed one test or procedure. They told Mrs. Rowe that big city doctors were always critical of community doctors and always tried to second-guess them in order to look good with families from outside the city.

Sean told the Rowes that it was typical for doctors to be defensive after they had been found to misdiagnose a case. They tried to shift blame elsewhere. Savin Medical was owned lock, stock, and barrel by Drs. Smith and Blade and had billed the Rowe's thousands of dollars for the useless lab tests. That was worth looking into, Sean thought.

But now it was time to be candid with Mr. and Mrs. Rowe about the case. He told them, "We need all of the early medical records covering the critical six-year period. Without these, I will have an impossible task in trying this case." Sean asked them if they had a copy of Lisa's medical records, dip stick, urine, and blood tests and studies from that time. Mrs. Rowe responded, "We requested the records before we saw Attorney McPherson. But

Dr. Smith and Dr. Blade said that the records had
been sent to Pediatric Hospital. When we later
checked with Pediatric Hospital, they said they
never received the records. After we filed suit, we
were told that, because we had a suit, they wouldn't
send the records unless approved by Attorney
Howe, the defense attorney." The Rowes indicated
that when they had asked Quigley about the records,
he said he would get a court order but, when they
called him about it, he simply told them it was on
the agenda and he was getting to it. The next time
they called him, he said that Sean was handling the
case and had total responsibility for obtaining the
records and that he would not be involved any
longer. He said that if the Rowes had any problems,
they should look to Sean.

Quigley had never asked for a court order to
get copies of the missing medical records. In fact,
for nearly three years, he had not done any
meaningful discovery on the case. Now it was
much too late. Sean told the Rowes, "I'll do my
best but if I can't get the medical records now, at
least I'll subpoena them for trial." He knew that
Howe would do everything possible to prevent him
from reviewing the medical records prior to the trial
date and Sean thought that he might not be able to
see the records at all until he put both Drs. Smith
and Savin on the witness stand. Then it might be

too late. He tried to brace the Rowes psychologically and told them to keep the faith. He said he would keep Lisa and them in his prayers and that he truly admired Lisa and would fight for her despite the odds.

Sean liked to end a client meeting on a positive note. For the first time that day, he saw both Mr. and Mrs. Rowe smile. He hoped he had won the confidence and trust of his clients. He explained that they would have to come to his office over the weekend in order to further answer Interrogatories, and that, in the meantime, he would be attempting to find competent medical experts to support the case. "If we fail to get the necessary medical experts, the case will have to be dismissed. But I'll do my best." Before they left, he shook Mr. Rowe's hand and he smiled for the first time. He gave Mrs. Rowe a hug. She seemed much happier than when she had entered the office. He also gave Lisa a big hug and a kiss on the forehead, and a miniature shamrock for luck. Sean promised he would do everything possible to help her. Lisa's handshake was weak, but her beautiful smile warmed Sean's heart.

After the Rowes left the office, Sean reflected and hoped that he had not in any way misled his clients and given them false hope. He thought that, under the circumstances, he had handled it correctly. He didn't want them to become demoralized before the trial because that could cause serious psychological damage – the kind that could derail the case. Sean vowed that under no circumstances would he give up. He would spend the days ahead thinking and strategizing how to win Lisa's case and he would fight for her with every ounce of his legal skill and ability. This could be the most important case of his life and Sean knew that by repeating to himself that he would fight hard no matter what the odds, he was not only psyching the Rowes for the upcoming battle, but he was preparing himself as well for the ordeal that surely awaited him in court.

That evening at home Sean felt closer to his wife and children than he had ever felt before. He was so grateful that God had blessed Miriam and him with two beautiful healthy children. He realized how lucky he was to have such a devoted wife and such wonderful kids. Sean thought about the courage, dedication, and selflessness of parents who care for extremely ill children. He wondered how they cope with the tremendous burden of caring for very sick children twenty-four hours a day, year in and year out. Their love was constant. Sean always tried to empathize with the pain and suffering of his clients. He felt he could not truly represent them before a jury unless he lived and touched their suffering and understood the depth of their emotional and physical pain.

The next morning, he headed for court filled with optimism and confidence. He realized the trial would likely be an ordeal, but he was determined not to be diffident, tentative, or pessimistic. He believed that confidence creates hope, hope creates opportunity, and opportunity wins cases.

He steeled himself to meet every problem with a strong spirit and determined effort. He wanted to make a strong first impression on the team of paralegals and lawyers from Howe and Gates. Using his body language and radiating confidence, he wanted to convey to Howe and Gates that he knew their doctors had malpracticed his young client, and he was ready to prove it to a jury. Sean knew that the stakes were enormous but he was ready to present his case and go to verdict. Somehow, Sean would give Lisa her day in court.

Chapter 7

The Pre-Trial Conference

Sean made it a point to get to the courtroom at least an hour early. He knew Judge Taylor was unforgiving and fanatic about adhering to the schedule. He had a reputation of defaulting and dismissing cases if the plaintiffs were only one minute late and Sean was not about to give Judge Taylor this opportunity to derail his case. He had the book on Judge Taylor and knew all his tricks.

Sean glanced into the swarm of paralegals and junior lawyers and, in their midst, presiding and accepting the adoration of all, was Attorney Chauncy Howe. Sean deliberately avoided eye contact. He walked by the menagerie and headed directly to the front of the courtroom. He wanted to create an atmosphere of determination and total preparation and to look as if he were supremely confident and totally prepared.

Sean observed that the Howe and Gates legal team wore their traditional court uniforms, dark blue pin-striped suits, stark white shirts, crimson and blue bow ties, and multi-colored suspenders. These school colors, Harvard crimson and Yale blue, conveyed a message to all, and particularly to Judge Taylor, that they were from the right schools, the right side of the track, and had the proper legal lineage. Judge Taylor himself always wore his crimson bow tie so the Howe and Gates uniform would certainly make the right first impression and win his approval.

Sean could tell immediately that the deck was well stacked against him. This courtroom was as hostile as was possible toward his client and toward him. He was not one of the State Street gang, the big law firms, and was out of his element in this battle. Judge Taylor was aligned by lineage, education, training, and practice with the corporate culture of Howe and Gates and he never identified with the underdog. Sean didn't expect him to start now. This was going to be the case of his life, and Sean knew it.

To counter Howe and Gates' large legal team, Sean, with great flair and serious demeanor, carried two large briefcases to his counsel table. It took several trips to carry all his "trial material" to the front and he made it a point to brush by the defense team and be certain that they were aware of his activity. A hush descended on the Howe and Gates team each time he walked by with another huge file.

Of course Sean was bluffing. In fact, the files and documents he brought to court were from the Federal Court incubator case and only the labels had been changed to read "Rowe Medical Case."

Like a good poker player, Sean was trying to impress all on the first hand. His tactics were working and he could sense that the Howe and Gates defense team was beginning to worry.

Eventually Chauncy Howe sauntered to the front of the courtroom, followed by his disciples, a team of six lawyers and six paralegals, a mix of male and female bright young faces. He nodded to Sean at counsel table and Sean nodded back. The psychological war had begun, a nod for a nod, an eye for an eye. Sean thought if he doesn't recognize me, why should I recognize him?

It was apparent from the body language and demeanor of both Sean and Chauncy Howe that they had little respect for one another. They were opposites in upbringing and education. Howe represented the State Street firm, the establishment, the corporate America law firm with extensive legal and political connections, attorneys who would use every tricky tactic, however bizarre, to win the case. To them, the end justified any means. Sean never trusted these large firms. He knew they were goal-orientated and would fight to win at any cost. They had to be watched at all times.

Judge Taylor, fastidious to the appointed time, bolted into the courtroom promptly at 9:00 A.M., banging the chamber door as he shot like a cannonball to the bench. He slammed his large black notebook down with a **CRACK!!** It sounded like an artillery barrage. Judge Taylor relished his dramatic entrances. The slamming and banging were meant to intimidate and always had the desired effect. The courtroom suddenly became stone silent.

The judge quickly searched through the stack of files on his desk and asked for the counsel on the Rowe case. Sean and Attorney Howe rose and approached the bench. Judge Taylor frowned when he saw Sean and glowered at him for what seemed like an eternity. Then, turning away he said, "Chauncy, I saw your partner, Bill, at our last Harvard reunion. Is there any problem for your clients with the assigned trial date?" Howe smiled knowingly, nodded at Judge Taylor and said smoothly, "All the defendants are not only ready, but eager for trial. They want this case tried at the earliest possible moment. It has caused great stress and embarrassment to two prominent physicians, Dr. Smith and Dr. Blade, and to a well-known and well-respected institution, Savin Medical. The earlier this case is tried, the better. The case as it now stands is totally frivolous and my clients are eager to move forward."

Turning to Sean, Judge Taylor blurted out in an angry rasp, "Is the plaintiff ready for trial on the case assigned?" Sean, as calmly as he could, told

Judge Taylor that his thirteen-year-old client, Lisa, was scheduled for a second dialysis treatment within the next two months and asked the court if the case could be continued for four months because of her medical condition. Judge Taylor glared at Sean, his white hair disheveled (he never seemed to comb it), his florid face more red than usual, his piercing eyes blinking rapidly. He was not pleased at Sean's request.

Judge Taylor finally shouted, "Request denied! Mr. McArthur, you know better than to ask for a last minute continuance! You have been in my courtroom before. I believe in timeliness in all court matters. We always try court cases on schedule in my courtroom. We honor time standards. We do not allow unprepared personal injury attorneys leave to casually extend trial dates forever." The tirade continued, "In my court, as you well know, there will be no continuances of an assigned trial date. You have brought a very serious malpractice case against two outstanding doctors and one of the best HMO clinics in Boston and you want these outstanding doctors to suffer another needless two-month delay for you to do some last-minute trial preparation. No, I will not allow you to do this, Mr. McArthur, not in my courtroom! You may get away with these questionable trial tactics with some of the newly appointed liberal inexperienced judges but not in my courtroom. Do you understand?"

Sean merely stood there stunned at the outburst. He did not say a word and merely nodded but his demeanor showed that he was hurt. Any further words would only add gasoline to the fire, which was already out of control. Taylor was already in a rage and Sean was only hoping that he did not suffer any more professional damage because of the judge's ranting and raving. Attorney Howe interrupted, "My clients are even considering counter-suing the plaintiffs." Judge Taylor continued, "Mr. Howe, you are right. A counter-suit may be in order. I can see by the very limited pleadings and discovery that there has hardly been any real work done by the plaintiff's attorney. Mr. McArthur, have you taken the depositions of Dr. Smith or Dr. Blade?"

"No, your honor."

Judge Taylor: "You mean you intend to engage in a highly technical medical case and you have not even taken the doctors' depositions? Mr. McArthur, that, to me, borders on total incompetent and unprofessional conduct and, after this trial is concluded, I shall immediately report you and your associate, Quigley McPherson, to the Board of Bar Overseers for potential disbarment!" Sean again stood stunned and speechless, totally humiliated.

Judge Taylor was chastising and sanctioning him for a case in which he only recently became involved.

But the judge was not finished; he was on a roll. Taylor could tell that Sean's case wasn't ready. "Mr. McArthur, have you ordered and received Dr. Smith's, Dr. Blade's and Savin Medical's records?"

"No, your honor."

"I cannot believe what you're saying to me! You are totally unprepared and you have not represented your clients well. You and Attorney McPherson have not done basic discovery. You are not in a position to prove a medical case based on the record before me. If you lose this case, I will recommend that your clients bring an immediate malpractice case against both of you for incompetence. You had better notify your malpractice carrier. Do you get my drift, Mr. McArthur?"

"Yes, Your honor." Sean felt faint and knew he could not defend Quigley's lack of preparation. He was in a desperate situation.

Judge Taylor continued, "I order this case to be tried not in two months but in two weeks. I require and order that you, Mr. McArthur, formally identify all of your medical experts and provide the court and defense counsel with detailed substance of their testimony within one week. Failure on your part to identify your medical experts and to provide details of their testimony will result in my disallowing their testimony at trial. I want them identified in one week."

Sean replied weakly "Yes, your honor." His weak voice betrayed his now total lack of confidence. He knew he was being systematically destroyed in the courtroom in front of members of the bar. But he also knew that the most important tactic was not to lose control or do anything further to infuriate an already out-of-control judge.

Judge Taylor: "I also deny your late filed Motion to Amend the Rowe Complaint as being totally untimely. I require you to supplement your client's answers to Interrogatories within one week as your client's answers are evasive and unresponsive. Mr. Howe, do you object to any of my orders; do you want them further supplemented, or do you have any further requests?"

Attorney Howe, during this tantrum, stood smiling contentedly, occasionally glancing back at the courtroom, nodding to the spectators and lawyers. He was fully enjoying Sean's embarrassment and humiliation. "Your honor," he said, "I find all your rulings totally appropriate, sound, and judicial. I would also like to advise the court that if Mr. McArthur does not comply to the letter with the court's rational and wise and very fair and equitable judicial orders, I shall move to dismiss this obviously frivolous malpractice case prior to the day of trial and prior to any witnesses being called."

Judge Taylor continued to roll along: "I am truly quite upset. I find it difficult to fathom that an attorney like Mr. McArthur would ever present such a poorly prepared case, not only in my court but in any court in the Commonwealth of Massachusetts. Do you understand my order, Mr. McArthur, and the gravity of the disposition of the case if you fail to meet these terms to the letter?"

"Yes, your honor," Sean managed to reply.

Sean turned to step away from the bench. Like a badly wounded soldier, he wanted to find some cover within the wide space of the courtroom. Instead, he faced the lawyers who were waiting their turn to face the judge. Their eyes were blank and unsympathetic. Sean knew he had been totally humiliated, dissected, and humbled before his peers and the lay people sitting in the courtroom. His proud trial reputation had probably been irreparably tarnished.

"Well," he thought, "Now I'm not only trying this case for Lisa, but I'm also trying it to protect my career and reputation. If I lose this case, I'll probably be disbarred, and will likely have a malpractice case launched against me to boot." The stakes were getting higher at each twist and turn of the case while the situation was becoming more dire and the chances of winning more distant. "How did I ever get into this mess?" he said to himself as he gathered up his files. In the past, he had handled many difficult and complex cases in which he bore the brunt of personal assaults and attacks on his trial ability by mean-spirited judges. But, this unabashed, hatred and anger hurled at him by an enraged Judge Taylor was by far the worst.

Sean's successes would be history if Judge Taylor dismissed this case and reported him for disbarment. He was afraid that his entire career was shattering before him simply because he had assumed the responsibility of handling a case that was mismanaged and unprepared by his associate. Sean's thoughts drifted to Quigley, who was in London, probably drinking and having a great time, totally oblivious to the disaster at hand. Sean said a silent prayer, "Please give me the strength, God. Give Lisa her jury trial."

He didn't remember how he finally managed to escape from the courtroom and get to his car. It was all a blur. It felt like he had been hit on the head and knocked semi-conscious. His brain felt traumatized and he was in a disoriented fog. He did remember that several spectators in the courtroom giggled and smiled at him derisively as he passed on his way out. When he made eye contact at all, it was met with a frozen unfriendly stare. He had never felt so embarrassed.

To tell the truth, Sean felt like he was having a nervous breakdown. So many conflicting thoughts buzzed through his head that his mind was becoming numb. He now knew how criminal defendants felt when they were escorted in shackles in and out of the courtroom like wild beasts. At times like this he wished he were anything but a lawyer. He wondered what he would tell Miriam, and how he could explain that his whole legal career was now riding on this one case. He knew Miriam would question why he took on this disaster.

He sat quietly in his car, on the verge of a great depression. His confidence level was at an all-time low. His paranoia about the medical and State Street establishment targeting him as a threat seemed to be winning out. Of course, it wasn't really paranoia if it actually occurred. Sean realized that he was now the bull's eye, definitely not the arrow. He was not on the attack but was on the run.

"Maybe," he thought, "I've succeeded too well." In a short time he had discovered yet another serious level of incompetence in greater Boston's doctors and hospitals. But he knew he was just trying to buttress his flagging confidence. He remembered the advice of one of his law professors. "To accomplish the impossible in the future, you must remember how you accomplished the possible in the past." So Sean mentally listed his past trial successes in an effort to bolster his fading confidence.

Of course, he immediately noted the Worcester case ordered a local community hospital to close until all of its defective incubators were repaired or replaced. He thought about the numerous breast cancer cases he had won, which made physicians and insurance companies think twice before refusing to perform tissue biopsy or ultrasound on persistent breast lumps. He thought about the radiological clinic, Chauncy Howe's former client, that he helped to close down. And there were the earlier cases; the anesthesiologist who he finally had suspended after his incompetence led to several patient deaths, the doctor who was suspended for taking drugs and for not following up after positive x-rays indicated lung cancer in a client who smoked. He repeated to himself, "Remember the past; look to the future."

Maybe it wasn't happenstance that early morning calls had disrupted his sleep over the last several cases. It was dawning on him that the current wave of malpractice suits against plaintiff's attorneys seemed too orchestrated to be coincidental. Of course, there **never** was a favorable medical verdict in Judge Taylor's court. The judge seemed to be doing everything he could to destroy plaintiff's cases. How could any trial attorney win a case in such a hostile and partisan environment?

Sean's thoughts drifted to the victory party at The 21st. "Why did I ever have that second Guinness?" he asked himself again. He vowed never again to make a major career-altering decision after a Guinness. It really was the "curse of the Irish." Sean chuckled to himself and realized that his spirit was restored. He had the heart of a fighter and this was no time to retreat. He would persevere. He remembered the legend of Irish chieftains – when too old to fight, they would dive onto their sword. They accepted the challenge. Facing Judge Taylor could not be worse than falling on your own sword! Sean laughed out loud. His fighting spirit had returned-he was back in the war!

He dropped by his office after the debacle at court. On his desk was a postcard with a picture of Buckingham Castle. He read, "After you win Lisa's case, why not join me in London? If you need help, call the Barrister Hotel. Good luck and top of the afternoon to you!" It was signed, "Big A". The office was empty except for the clatter of a lone typewriter. Rosie was also out of town, shopping in New York and enjoying the night life. You could count on Rosie and Quigley not to be there when it mattered. Thank heavens Sean never depended on them to prepare cases.

Sean was on count down, starting from scratch, and he knew it. He had one week to find the necessary medical witnesses. Where to begin? On his desk sat Lisa's medical record from Pediatric Hospital and Sean quickly went through it. It was quite detailed and described each diagnostic and kidney test that showed the extent of Lisa's kidney damage. Her prognosis was very bad. Unless a donor was found soon, she would certainly die.

Chapter 8

Medical Miracles

Sean was desperate and needed help fast. If he didn't engage an expert immediately, he would lose the case. He dialed Pediatric Hospital and asked to speak to Dr. Grouper, the nephrologist, who was in charge of the Nephrology Department. After waiting for what seemed like forever, he heard, "Dr. Grouper. How can I help you?" Sean identified himself as the attorney who was trying to help Lisa in her case and said that he needed to learn as much as he could about her condition. He explained that the lawyer previously handling the case had neglected it to the point that it required preparation from scratch and with the trial coming up in two weeks, he needed expert testimony about Lisa's damaged kidneys.

Wasting no time on pleasantries, Sean asked, "Doctor, I know this is short notice but, would you be able to testify two weeks from now concerning Lisa's kidney complication and her prognosis?" After a pause, Grouper answered, "I would love to help Lisa. She is a beautiful and very brave little girl and I feel very sorry about her condition. But, that week is impossible for me. I'm the lead speaker for an international seminar scheduled that week in London. It's sponsored by the British Medical Society and has been in the planning for three years. I've been committed for several years and simply can't miss it. If you can put your case over to the week after, I would have no problem."

Sean felt like he had been hit by a ten-ton brick. He was heartbroken but didn't want to sound defeated. In the calmest voice possible he said, "Judge Taylor is an angry judge and vowed not to allow any continuances. However, if you can't make it next week, could Dr. Hamilton assist Lisa on this case?" Sean deliberately used Lisa's name to show his close identity with her. He was aware that Grouper and Hamilton, his assistant, were very fond of Lisa and he hoped this would influence the decision in his favor.

Dr. Grouper replied, "I'll check with Bill. We're understaffed at the clinic due to HMO cutbacks, but I'll ask him to give you a call. I know he's very fond of Lisa, as I am, and has been with her throughout her ordeal. Dr. Hamilton has only been with me for six months, but Lisa was one of his first patients so he knows her case very well. He is young, extremely bright, and very dedicated, and I know he'll want to do the best he can to help Lisa. In fact, hold on a second and I'll try to buzz his line and introduce you to Bill right now."

Sean waited then heard a few clicks and thought the line was dead. But then he heard Dr. Grouper's voice: "Bill, I have Lisa's attorney, Sean McArthur, on the phone. He needs some assistance on Lisa's litigation case. Would you speak to him?" He heard Hamilton say, "Certainly," right before he came on the line and said, "Hello? This is Bill Hamilton." Sean's voice shook a little as he reiterated his request: "Dr. Hamilton, because of Dr. Grouper's commitment to the international conference, would you be able to pinch hit for him and testify in court about Lisa's deteriorating kidney condition, complications, and prognosis?"

Dr. Hamilton's reply, in a pleasant and reassuring voice, was immediate and emphatic: "Yes, I would be very happy to testify. I admire Lisa and am continually moved by her courage. And I'm appalled at the level of pediatric care she received before coming to us. Unfortunately, I've seen first-hand the suffering she and her family have gone through. The damage to her kidneys is irreversible. Sadly, unless she receives a kidney donation soon, my prognosis is that she will be dead within six months. Her situation is desperate."

Hamilton stated he had not seen Dr. Smith's or Dr. Blade's medical records or any of the diagnostic test results from Savin Medical, although he and Dr. Grouper repeatedly had requested these records. He explained that it was very unusual for treating physicians not to cooperate with Pediatric Hospital and to send records immediately, particularly when the patient was in a life-threatening condition. He remembered receiving a letter from some attorneys in Boston after he had made repeated requests for the records. They said no records would be forwarded because a potential litigation was pending.

Sean's heart was pounding. Hamilton was very critical of the level of care administered by Lisa's treating physicians, so he plunged in and explicitly asked the doctor the most critical question. "Should Drs. Smith or Blade have been able to diagnose Lisa's infected kidney some time over the six-year period, before she was admitted to Pediatric Hospital in such poor condition?"

Without hesitation, Hamilton said, "Absolutely! Lisa's kidneys were so terribly infected when we first saw her that we were able to diagnose her condition after one simple test. They had to have been chronically or continually infected over that six-year period. It takes quite a while before an infection can destroy both kidneys. It's my opinion that Lisa's one kidney had been infected over that six-year period and I'm very sure that if you checked the urine studies done during that time, they would have to show some positive tests for

protein and infection. Furthermore, in my opinion
the dip stick method of testing is not state-of-the-art
but is outmoded and unreliable. I can't believe that
urine tests taken during Lisa's previous treatment
would be anything but positive in some instances.
For you to win the case, all you have to do is check
the urine studies. They will substantiate the prior
kidney damage. Furthermore, the damage should
have been picked up by both Dr. Blade and Dr.
Smith and I can't see how they missed it."

Hamilton was obviously outraged. His
voice rose as he continued: "If this case was on my
recent board examination and the facts were
presented as this case is detailed, it would be a gross
departure from accepted pediatric and urology
standards for both Smith and Blade to have
overlooked the diagnosis of early kidney disease.
In my opinion, these doctors, along with Savin
Medical, really missed the boat. This should not be
in litigation but before the Board of Medicine for
license suspension. I'm very upset with what
they've done, and I'm angry! I'll do anything to
help you with this case."

Sean was overjoyed and tried to keep his
voice steady while they wrapped up the
conversation. Now he had his expert and more!
Hamilton would also attest to the negligence of
Lisa's previous physicians. Sean didn't want to

push his luck so he immediately thanked Dr. Hamilton for his time and told him he would list him as his expert witness. They arranged to talk in a few days and scheduled an appointment so Sean could learn as much as possible about the intricacies of kidney disease. Hamilton said he would be more than pleased to instruct Sean as to kidneys and use the charts and material at Pediatric Hospital to help him understand the concepts of how kidneys deteriorate.

When Sean got off the phone, his hands were trembling and he had tears in his eyes. The pressure of the impending trial, the stress of Judge Taylor's orders, the whole case in general, all were nearly overwhelming. His thoughts turned to the upcoming trial. Would Hamilton be allowed to testify as a nephrologist against Smith and Dr. Blade, who were board certified pediatricians? He knew that Hamilton would be able to testify as to injury – the so-called damage and medical causation part of the case. However, what narrow ruling would Judge Taylor make to prevent Hamilton from testifying against a pediatrician? In Massachusetts, on the question of expert testimony, there was always a key issue subject to judicial discretion: The experts who testify against the defendant usually come from the same field of the defendant's specialty. There were rulings to the effect that on cross-specialty, a nephrologist, for instance, who would know about kidneys, could testify as to whether an injury was related to a pediatrician's treatment of the kidneys. But Sean knew that Judge Taylor, who was both conservative and restrictive as well as hostile in general, would not allow Hamilton to testify as a cross-expert. Just having Hamilton in his camp would be helpful on the question of damages but not on liability. In order to present this aspect of the case against Dr. Smith, Sean knew he would need a board certified pediatrician to testify. Where could he find a pediatric expert on such short notice?

As he sat thinking, Jennifer's voice came over the intercom. "Quigley's calling from London and wants to talk to you." On returning to the office, Sean had had the foresight to ask Quigley's secretary to ring him with the morning's results from the Pre-Trial conference. When he put the phone to his ear, he heard the ever-present pub noises and Irish music in the background. It was 10:30 P.M. London time and 5:30 P.M. in Boston. "Big A," Sean shouted into the din. "We are in real trouble! Judge Taylor is threatening both of us with disbarment. He's already reported us to the Board of Bar Overseers for the way we've handled this case so far. Taylor's also gone on record requesting that our clients sue us for incompetence if we don't prevail on this case. It's a real mess! I need a pediatrician to testify at trial. Do you know any pediatricians I can call? You told me at The 21st that you knew some doctors who could be helpful. If we don't engage a pediatrician within the week, our legal careers are probably finished forever!"

After this fierce harangue, Quigley's voice sounded weak and a bit woozy. "Don't worry so much, Sean. Taylor is an asshole. Yes, he's disbarred some lawyers and yes, we are in deep shit. But, I do know a pediatrician who's on loan at Tremont Hospital on a fellowship and who's conducting a special research project. He should be able to give us a hand. I also know his brother, Matt, who happens to be a bartender at The Barrister. I'll call Shamus O'Reilly and let him know we need his help. I'll explain our predicament and I'm sure he'll help. He's a good pal and I'm sure he won't disappoint me. He owes me a favor. Don't lose faith, Sean. Good luck and I'll call you after I make contact with him."

Sean felt some immediate relief. Maybe Quigley's friend could deliver. Reality, however, quickly intervened. His associate had a bad track record, and in the past many of his contacts had turned out to be unreliable and huge disappointments. Drinking buddies very rarely delivered.

As Sean drove home through the usual heavy traffic caused by the never ending Big Dig, he reviewed the day's activities. What a strange day. He started off, brave and confident, marching into court. Then, in one fell swoop, Judge Taylor shot his confidence full of holes and shredded his reputation in front of everyone. Now his legal reputation depended on winning Lisa's case. If he lost, both he and Quigley would likely be disbarred and would probably be sued by their own clients. What a mess! Now his hopes of winning the case rested on the shoulders of some unknown English doctor on a special project in Boston whose brother was a bartender in Quigley's pub in his timeshare in London. Sean's legal license to practice hinged on the caprice and whim of cronyism. Hope does spring eternal, but Sean, even though he was looking for a ray of sunshine, saw very little light in his immediate future. His situation was getting darker by the minute.

That night, he tossed and turned, an obvious tip-off to Miriam that the kidney case was not going well. Sean, as usual, tried not to discuss his cases at home. He didn't want to worry his wife needlessly. If she knew about this precarious situation, she too would be tossing and turning. Sean knew that over the next six days he must try to look, speak, and act with confidence. Sometimes, however, his physical being betrayed him. When he was in deep trouble and hurting, it showed in the way he spoke and moved. He developed a silent mantra: "Six days to go. The clock is ticking."

With his days and hours so numbered, Sean lived within the six-day time schedule, his whole life dictated by this case. Every second, all he could think about was Lisa's case. He tried desperately to stay calm, but would fly into a panic and curse to himself: "No lawyer should be under this totally unreasonable schedule." Sean tried to control his emotions and fears but all his meditation and psychological pep talks were not helping now. He was in a state of disarray with fear gnawing at the edges. Finding a competent pediatrician to testify seemed a real long shot.

The next day, Sean checked the answering service. Quigley had called and left his number. Sean dialed the overseas operator immediately. It was 8:00 P.M. at the Barrister Hotel in London and Sean again heard the clattering of the glasses and the loud Aussie and English songs in the background. To overcome the crowd noise, he shouted into the phone, "Big A, did you call Dr. O'Reilly? Is he with us? Can I call him?" He realized his voice sounded panicky and he regretted his lack of "cool," particularly in dealing with Quigley, who would sense it immediately.

However, he didn't care at this point. He wanted Quigley to feel the heat and the desperation, and the obvious potential dangers of their situation. He could hardly hear him over the bar din. "Quigley! Speak up! I can't hear a damn word you're saying!"

His nerves straining, he heard: "I contacted O'Reilly. He has excellent credentials and he's board certified to boot. He's been working with the Chief of Tremont Hospital for the last year. He's never testified in court but, as a favor to me and Matt, he said he would testify, if you absolutely need him. I assured him we did and that you would call him. Give him a call and, if you have any problems, call me. I'll be here at the bar all night." After giving Sean the doctor's private number, Quigley said, "Don't worry, Sean. We're in great shape. Remember it's not over until it's over."

Sean couldn't repress a smile. Quigley had a way of mixing quaint expressions with a touch of Yogi Berra which made for an interesting, if not comforting, sentiment.

Sean dialed Dr. O'Reilly's private home line. The phone rang several times then he heard: "Dr. O'Reilly speaking. May I help you?" Sean introduced himself and marveled at Dr. O'Reilly's sophisticated Irish accent. Sean explained the details of Lisa's case and the fact that she had very

likely been misdiagnosed by her two long-term
pediatrician and urologist. He went over her
medical history, emphasizing the alleged negative
dip stick tests and urine studies. He told O'Reilly
that he was unable to review the medical records
and tests of the treating doctors or Savin Medical,
and that the medical history he presented was
consistent with the history elicited by Lisa's
parents. The identical history was contained in the
records of Pediatric Hospital, where Lisa was now
being treated for kidney failure.

"May I call you Sean?" O'Reilly inquired.

"Of course. May I call you Shamus?"

"Certainly. First of all, any friend of Quigley's is a
friend of mine. Big A has helped me out of many
embarrassing moments. On the medical case, I find
it totally unbelievable that any physician worth his
salt could completely misdiagnose a deteriorating
kidney condition for a six-year period. This is
unbelievable and, if it happened, it is totally
improper and terrible medicine. Furthermore, no
child could lose both kidneys by infection without
some signs and symptoms. Lisa definitely, based
on what you just told me, had signs of infection.
Her frequent urination, her frequent thirst, her long
absences from school, her on-again, off-again
viruses are all consistent symptoms of potential
kidney disease. If you look at her urine tests, you

should find positive signs of protein in her urine. This is a classical sign of impending kidney failure. This is the 'gold standard,' if you will. It does confirm a kidney failure. When you get hold of those urine tests, you are bound to find some that are positive results. They just **have** to be there."

"Furthermore," he went on, "the dip stick test is totally discredited and any pediatrician who uses it is in the dark ages. Dip sticks are used by doctors who want to run up the bill. They can be inaccurate and unreliable, unlike urinalysis. Community doctors, such as Smith and Blade, who own the testing facility, don't like urinalysis because the profit margin on dip sticks is so much higher. I question any doctor with an understanding of kidney disease who would reasonably dispute this. If any doctor at my hospital or in the British Isles used this discredited method, I would testify against them and report them to the Board of Medicine.

Certainly I will help you. In fact, I'll do everything possible to assist you. I can't believe this case is in litigation. It should have been settled long ago."

Sean couldn't believe his ears. Dr. O'Reilly was the perfect expert witness. Not only was he highly qualified and willing to testify, he had no problem with the medical complexity of the case and was willing to attest to misdiagnosis. Sean could barely express his "thank you" out of his mouth, he was so excited. Trying to be cool and calm, he said, "Shamus, I do so appreciate your help. I'll send over all of Lisa's hospital records from Pediatric Hospital. I'm working closely with Dr. Hamilton who will also be testifying on Lisa's behalf."

"I do have to clear one thing, but it shouldn't be a problem," O'Reilly said. "I have to get my chief's permission to take time from the hospital. But, once I explain this situation to him, I know he'll support my involvement in your case. I have no doubt that he will give me the time in order to testify. He's a great guy and we work well together. If there are any glitches, give me your number so I can reach you."

Sean gave his office and home numbers and said again, "Thanks for your involvement. I should meet with you in a day or so and, in the meantime, I'll identify you as one of our medical experts. I'll stay in touch. Call me if you have any problems or need further information. I'll send you all the information I have right away."

Before ringing off, O'Reilly said, "Sean, after the defense attorneys know you have competent medical testimony from excellent hospitals, I know this case will never go to court. If it were being heard in England, it would have been settled years ago."

Sean replied, "Shamus, in a perfect world that would be true, but in Massachusetts, the same rules do not apply. Drs. Smith and Blade are well connected both medically and legally and they will fight hard. Doctors in the Massachusetts Medical Society play hard and tough and never admit fault. And medical insurers hate to give away the profits. Jamie, take my word for it, Lisa's case will never settle but will be tried to jury verdict. Thanks again for your support and, after this ordeal is over, let's go to a good London style pub and have a Bass or two or, better yet, some Murphy stout."

Sean put down the phone, amazed by his good fortune. He almost could not believe it. He wanted to jump up and down and scream for joy. In a few short strokes he went from the saddest lawyer in Boston to the happiest in the world. "Thank God." "Thank Quigley." He even thanked Bloody Old England and all his Irish ancestors.

"Now," Sean thought, "the plot thickens. Now there's a chance, however slight, of having a jury decide Lisa's case." Somehow, fate and the hands of the Almighty seemed to be moving the case towards a jury verdict. Fate and the hands of the Almighty seemed to be moving the case forward in her favor. The Gods were finally smiling on Lisa. There was hope.

Once again, however, Sean's exhilaration rode the rollercoaster up to great joy and down to numbing fear. The climb up was always tortuous and the giddy feeling short-lived. Murphy's Law applied. He remembered that everything right could suddenly go wrong. The fates were quick to change their minds.

He called London with the good news. Elated, Quigley crowed, "Now the bastards will have their trial!" Sean, "The only potential problem was clearing Dr. O'Reilly's schedule with his chief, but O'Reilly thought that was a mere technicality."

"Don't worry about that," Quigley said. "We now have them where we want them. O'Reilly is very bright and articulate. He'll make a great witness and the jury will love his cultivated Irish accent and engaging personality. He is pure gold and even though we have a terrible judge, we have a chance."

Sean said, "Big A, I would still be concerned with his chief's approval. Medicine has become very hostile to litigation and the teaching hospitals are making it more difficult for junior doctors to testify on malpractice cases."

"Don't worry Sean. You worry too much about details. O'Reilly will testify. List him as a witness and together with Hamilton, we're in business."

"O.K. Big A. Ask your buddies to sing a few songs for Lisa. I'll keep you updated."

Chapter 9

Momentum

In five days the names and detailed expected testimony of the plaintiff's experts had to be filed with the court and Sean was concerned. He hadn't met with his medical experts and worse, they hadn't yet reviewed the defendants' medical and physicians' records. He knew he could subpoena these records for the day of trial, but doing so at this late date would be resisted fiercely by Howe and his defense team.

Preparation and planning were key to a successful cross-examination. Sean definitely would have preferred to review and analyze Drs. Smith and Blade's records with his designated experts, Dr. O'Reilly and Dr. Hamilton prior to trial. As it now stood, their credibility before the jury would be severely diminished if they showed anything less than a complete and thorough understanding of Lisa's case. But this risk was inevitable; he would have to improvise. It was dangerous, but there was no other way – he would have to learn about the case from each person in the witness box as the trial proceeded. It would be like playing Russian Roulette.

The parent's recollection, even if buttressed by medical bills, personal checks, and itemized telephone calls, would not provide credible evidence of a misdiagnosis. And it was obvious that Judge Taylor would do his level best to humiliate Sean in front of the jury and to lecture him for wasting valuable time if he attempted to pause or take any recesses during the trial to study the medical records. Sean was caught in a desperate squeeze.

"We'll do the best with what we have," he decided. Strange things happen at trial and, even though he subscribed to the doctrine that trial work is "ninety-percent preparation and ten-percent improvisation," he had found that in close trials, just as in nail-biting sports events, last minute insights and shifts in strategy had won a hell of a lot of close cases.

He would have to pray for that proverbial Hail Mary pass. He remembered when Doug Flutie, a fellow Boston College alumnus, threw a winning pass for underdog Boston College against highly ranked Miami in the last second and against improbable odds. Sean was hoping that such a miracle could take place in the courtroom and not just on the football field.

"Well," he mused to himself. "It's time for positive thinking". To psyche himself for the upcoming trial, he ran through his favorite inspirational sayings: "where there is hope, there is life;" "make the impossible possible," "give it your best shot," "it's not over 'til it's over" "Never give up the ship." "Success is failure turned inside out."

He felt a little uplifted so he went back to considering his strategy. He would not wait to identify his medical experts until the day before Judge Taylor's deadline. He would certainly not wait until the very last day because you never know what can happen. He would not give himself a one-day buffer zone as Murphy's Law was still in effect. He was now intensely melancholy and guarded because he knew that, no matter what great trial strategy he planned, something could go wrong and often did. He realized that, in many ways, his superstitions were very similar to Quigley's, and that was distressing to him.

Presenting a complex medical case to an unsophisticated lay jury was a risk. He remembered great battles that were won or lost by famous military strategists simply because of happenstance. Napoleon was defeated at Waterloo, despite the element of surprise when attacking the English, because a rainstorm prevented him from properly positioning his heavy artillery. This delayed his surprise and allowed Wellington to reform and launch a deadly and successful counterattack. And, closer to home, General Lee lost a tactical advantage at Gettysburg because several of his field generals delayed seizing the high ground at Cemetery Hill in the early stages of the battle. The Confederates were forced to surrender the high ground to the Union, which lead to Pickett's desperate, costly and disastrous defeat on the decisive third day of battle.

Sean's mind was becoming distracted and he forced it back to the present. Now that he had two well qualified experts, Dr. O'Reilly and Dr. Hamilton. He now had the necessary expert witnesses to prove his case. It was time to move from strategy to action.

With the court deadline quickly approaching, Sean met with Dr. Hamilton and spent an educational session with him reviewing all aspects of the case. He particularly wanted to learn as much as he could about the intricacies and anatomy of the kidney and how it was slowly destroyed over a six-year period.

Sean noted how young Dr. Hamilton looked, and how boyish he was in many of his mannerisms. But though he looked more like a college senior than a board certified nephrologist, Dr. Hamilton was, in fact, one of the leading nephrologists in the country. Hamilton had a kind and gentle charm that immediately put anyone at ease and Sean could see why he was so successful with his young kidney patients. He had a caring and concerned manner and spoke in a polite and gentle way.

When Sean talked of Lisa, Dr. Hamilton become concerned and very alert. Sean could tell he had a powerful ally. As hard as he would fight for Lisa's life through litigation and trial, Hamilton would fight with all the weapons known to modern medicine to minimize her pain and suffering and to ensure her chance of surviving her deadly battle with kidney failure. While Sean was fighting Lisa's legal case, Dr. Hamilton was literally battling for her very life.

Hamilton repeated what he had said to Sean on the phone. "I can't believe that for six years her treating doctors never gave her a basic kidney evaluation! Lisa should have been referred to a nephrologist in the first year of her treatment, not the **sixth** year!" His tone gentled a bit when he spoke of Lisa's fifth grade teacher. "I'd like to meet Paula Murray some day and thank her for referring Lisa to our hospital. She must be a special person. If she had not referred Lisa to Pediatric Hospital, she would have died of her kidney complications already."

Hamilton shook his head while he spoke. "Lisa's medical history showed the classic signs and symptoms of kidney infection. Any well-trained pediatrician should have known this. Sean, please get those urine studies and I guarantee you'll find a history of protein in the urine. This is a classic sign of kidney infection and it would **have** to show up in the urine tests."

He continued, his voice rising urgently, "Lisa's kidneys could not have deteriorated so rapidly without **some** evidence of protein in the urine. Sean, you have to do the best you can and get those studies! Even though dip stick tests are not the best diagnostic study available, they'll win the case for you or lose it if you don't." Then he launched into a tirade directed at self-serving doctors. "The only doctors using dip stick tests these days are just trying to make a few bucks. They refuse to refer very sick patients to teaching hospitals because they don't want to lose the income, especially from their own lab work. It's mercenary and it's costing people their lives. Once their kidneys are destroyed, the government has to pay dialysis three times a week, and the patients pay in suffering for the rest of their lives. This is truly unethical and cruel!"

Sean, who usually was affable and hardly ever short on words, sat speechless. Hamilton had just read the medical riot act and, in no uncertain terms, accused Smith, Blade, and Savin Medical of gross medical incompetence, with greed as their motivation. Sean recognized that if Judge Taylor allowed Hamilton to testify, the case would definitely reach the jury and Lisa would have some hope, at least, of a favorable verdict. "You **have** got to get those medical records, particularly those urine studies. The studies will, without question, show protein in the urine and if they don't, I guarantee they're unreliable or they've been altered."

At this last comment, Sean audibly gasped. Would Chauncy Howe and the high-powered clients knowingly withhold critical records or alter and falsify the originals in order to protect their careers and reputations? If this were so, and he could prove the records were altered, that would be potentially criminal for all concerned. It could lead to the revocation of Smith and Blade's medical licenses, the closing down of the Savin Medical Clinic, and potential Bar proceedings against them. Sean knew he was getting ahead of himself. The case was heating up and his adrenaline was surging.

Sean spent the rest of the afternoon reviewing the diagrams and exhibits with Hamilton. The young doctor would make a great witness. He knew how to make complex terms very simple and understandable to a lay person. His work on the Indian reservation had contributed to the very special and easy way he had of communicating with non-medical people. He had the common touch.

Sean was very pleased with Hamilton's unselfish commitment to the pending litigation. Hamilton knew, with certainty, that Lisa's medical expenses would continue to grow and she would need hundreds of thousands of dollars to fund her treatments. He feared for Lisa's future if Sean did not win the case.

After his intense session with Dr. Hamilton, Sean felt he had learned more about kidneys in those few hours than in all the time he devoted to reading medical books and treatises. Hamilton truly was one of the best teachers he had ever met. Sean felt confident that he could explain Lisa's case precisely and in layman's terms to the jury. He had identified the particular areas of misdiagnosis and neglect committed by Drs. Smith and Blade. Sean, too, was now clear about which medical points he would emphasize in cross-examination.

Sean went back to his office feeling confident. He spent six hours writing down, in great detail, what the expected testimony of both his medical experts would be at trial. He wanted all his written discovery responses filed in court to be full, complete, and extremely detailed. He incorporated as much medical jargon and technical language as he could. He knew Judge Taylor was ignorant of medical technicalities. The judge, therefore, would not be able to dismiss the expert Answers for being technically incorrect.

After he finished writing the plaintiff's expert answer to questions submitted by the defendant doctors, Sean knew that even Judge Taylor would have to accept their detailed responses as being legally and medically correct. The plaintiff's detailed responses covered six pages and included precise medical terminology and language and read like a treatise or a medical textbook. After it was typed, Sean called the Rowes and arranged to meet with them on his way to the courthouse so they could sign the expert Answers. Then, armed with the necessary legal documents, Sean took a cab to his clients' home for their signatures and then continued to the Middlesex County courthouse.

At the courthouse law library, he made copies of the plaintiff's expert answers. Then he delivered the original documents in hand to Ed Sheridan, Judge Taylor's clerk.

Sean had a special respect for Ed. Over the years, Sean and Ed had developed a warm friendship and Ed had always been helpful to Sean. Ed was a frustrated trial attorney and might well have made a great trial lawyer. He had a sharp legal mind and could read people very well, instantly identifying the "good, the bad, and the ugly." Ed once had told Sean that he admired "his guts and tenaciousness in the courtroom" and his "determination to go the last mile for his client."

Ed had been Sean's trial clerk when he won his very first major medical malpractice case and Sean felt very comfortable with him. Ed asked, "Have you recovered from Taylor's explosion?"

Sean answered, "I don't think anyone ever does, but I know if I misstep along the way, he'll dismiss my case. That's actually why I'm here, Ed. I'm deadly afraid of being torpedoed by Judge Taylor's biases. I have the court-stamped plaintiff's Answers of designated experts to all the defendants' Interrogatories as well as the plaintiff's Supplemental Answers to their Interrogatories right here."

Ed glanced at the stack of papers as Sean went on: "Ed, could you do me a great favor and deliver this, in hand, to my good friend, the ever-smiling and benevolent Judge Taylor? All of the documents have been docketed in the court docket book. I'm doing everything by the book. I'll deliver these copies to the loveable and equally friendly Chauncy Howe on my way back to my office. Could you do me this favor, Ed?"

"Sean, amigo, I remember your first case before Judge Todd. I remember it well. Is that anesthesiologist still blowing out lungs or has he been put out to pasture? Your case was one of the first six-figure medical verdicts ever in our court. Haven't been too many since you know. Maybe this will be your next one."

Ed flipped through the court documents and said, "I've glanced over your Answers. You have great experts and lots of medical terms. Judge Taylor, who I don't think has the best eyesight, will have to read this with a medical dictionary. You were right on target to use so much medical terminology. It may prevent a dismissal. As always, good strategy."

Sean, "Big A and I are fighting for our legal lives and I'm trying to win a case without access to the defendants' medical and hospital records. At trial, I'll subpoena Dr. Smith, Dr. Blade, and Savin Medical's records. Ed, I'd appreciate it if you would guard those records with your life. You, of all people, know that some records are mysteriously lost in the courtroom. I've lost a few cases that way due to the last minute missing records and I don't want to have this one stolen from me. To tell you the truth, Ed, instinctively I don't trust Howe and Gates, the defense team, one iota. They will do anything to win. The end justifies the means in their minds. A bright young eager beaver might be looking to advance to partnership quickly. If you get a chance, keep an eye on Howe's slippery defense team. You've given me help in the past and I certainly will need your support this time around."

"Seanboy, keep cool! Remember, hit the jury with the facts. Keep it simple. Too many medical lawyers make a simple case complex. Don't make that mistake. Remember the definition KISS. Keep it simple, stupid! Not bad advice in a medical case. Good luck and I know you'll do well."

"Thanks Ed. I'll need all the good luck I can muster. I hope Irish eyes will smile on Lisa." Sean left Ed with an Irish theme because he knew Ed and his wife made a trip to the Old Sod every three years to visit with Ed's Irish relatives. Ed loved anything Irish, especially Irish history. Sean felt relieved, like a little of the burden had been shifted from his shoulders. He was making positive progress on the case.

In the courthouse corridors, Sean bumped into several classmates from Boston College Law School. He always enjoyed the collegiality and fun he had with former classmates, and loved to reminisce with them about their law school ordeal and how "we few good men" somehow survived one of the toughest law schools in the country. In the sixties, BC only graduated one out of three law students. Talk about a Marine Boot Camp!

Sean was able to bum a ride into Boston with one of his former classmates. They spent the short trip to Boston talking about the "good old days," which he knew were actually hell and the toughest three years of his life. At 28 State Street, one of the tallest skyscrapers in the center of Boston, Sean quickly rode the elevator all the way up to Howe and Gates, on the top floor, the prestigious penthouse suite.

Only the very senior and most successful partners of the highest financial standing in the pecking order of the law firm of Howe and Gates resided in these ornate and impressive penthouse suites. Sean entered the well-appointed reception area whose color and design reflected a palatial setting. Everything in the office was elaborately decorated blue, mahogany and cherry wood seemed to be the theme. He immediately was impressed with the gleaming dark blue leather chairs, the cherry wood furniture and conference table, and the marvelous Picasso and Monet impressionist paintings hung throughout the conference room. As he approached the receptionist, Sean could see into the impressive large, windowed conference room. A long dark conference room table was covered with numerous files, papers, medical blow-ups, and books. Through the open glass, he could see

Chauncy Howe and his legal minions pouring over the files and medical treatises.

Sean realized that he had caught Howe and Gates actually putting in some honest hours into their time charges for the up-and-coming kidney trial. This time, Sean would not be trying his case against an unseasoned and unprepared defense counsel, and he knew it. He could see with his own eyes that the Howe and Gates team was deeply involved in preparing this case. Chauncy Howe had the brightest of the bright helping him – all high-standing Ivy League law school graduates. Howe had the best legal weapons at his disposal and knew how to use them well.

Sean was intrigued, as always, by the steady rainbow-like blur made by the colorful Brooks Brothers bow ties and suspenders of Chauncy Howe's supporting cast. Sean thought the Howe team was dressed for a musical play rather than for a major medical trial. Standing in the reception area, he vividly recalled again the ridicule and deep hurt he had endured long ago at the hands of the junior partner while interviewing at a similar prestigious State Street law firm.

Sean's mind quickly reverted to the present. As he approached the beautiful and smartly attired receptionist, he recognized Chauncy Howe's senior partner and older brother, Jonathan, casually standing outside his office puffing on his trademark corn pipe. Jonathan was in his early fifties and the son of the founder, Simon Howe, had a deep tan from his latest Caribbean vacation and was known for his expertise in corporate tax matters. Sean approached him: "Jonathan, I'm on a case with your brother, Chauncy. He wanted these executed Answers. Would you sign for them?"

Jonathan, ever so polite and professional, and not recognizing Sean as an attorney, responded, "Sure. I'll sign the receipt," and he scribbled his signature only two letters of which one could decipher, the J and the H. This was all Sean needed. Now Attorney Howe would not be able to deny that he received the executed Answers days **before** Judge Taylor's imposed deadline.

Sean smiled and felt a sense of great exhilaration as he rode down the penthouse elevator. He instinctively looked around checking for the listening devices on the elevator as he knew were there but did not find any at the time. Sean knew that many an important litigation case was lost because of stupid casual and damaging remarks made by litigants or attorneys who thought they had the confidentiality of an untapped elevator. Howe and Gates knew all the tricks and, when dealing with them, Sean had to keep his head up at all times.

Chapter 10

Pre-Trial Maneuverings

The day after Sean delivered the documents to Howe and Gates and filed them in court, he received, in turn, a large bulky UPS package from his opponents. In it, they had set forth every conceivable last minute defense motion including a Motion to Dismiss all Defendants, Motion to limit Sean's opening to fifteen minutes, Motion to strike demonstrative charts and articles, Motion to exclude plaintiff's evidence. The list went on and on. Their expert Answers identified three prominent pediatricians, three outstanding urologists, and three nephrologists, all associated with leading Boston hospitals and all with impressive medical credentials.

Sean could easily see that the defendant's experts were the best of the best. They each had an impressive teaching and clinical background, were well written in their field, and all were professionals of impeccable medical background and experience. These experts would be entirely credible and certainly would impress the jury. As he reviewed the documents, Sean knew these witnesses could never be impeached on their outstanding qualifications or credentials. His only hope was to somehow get them to agree with him on the plaintiff's medical contentions.

He wasn't sure how he would accomplish this, but he had a secret weapon that had worked for him in the past. He would look for a flaw in the defendants' medical records and have their own experts agree that, because of this flaw, their treatment did not meet the standards of care in their field of specialty. Conducting an effective cross-examination would be difficult because his knowledge of the particulars in the case was limited. That worried him. But the experts' credentials didn't necessarily intimidate him. It was not the quantity or number of experts arrayed against his client but the quality of the experts. And, on the face of it, these certainly had quality. He desperately needed Lisa's medical records but how could he get them?

Sean had returned to his office determined to persevere. He would, as he kept saying to psyche himself for the encounter, do his best. But even though he questioned whether his best would be good enough, he vowed to fight to the end and give the defendants a run for their money. He knew he could control **his** case, but he could not control the defense.

Over the last several weeks, as he had become intensely involved with the Rowe case, he had stopped attending the weekly Friday meeting with Rosie. Rosie's world had not changed. He still had his Friday cocktail and gifts and flowers still arrived from his many admirers. It seemed, however, that Rosie was becoming a little upset now that Sean was devoting all his working hours to Lisa's case. It was obvious that Sean was giving more time to Quigley's case than the other cases referred by Rosie, and Sean sensed his resentment. Rosie particularly disliked the kidney case because he knew he wouldn't share any fee if it produced a favorable settlement or verdict. He increasingly nagged Sean about why he didn't try to settle Lisa's case for small money so he could work on some "winning medical cases."

At the office, Sean gave Rosie a general, and very sketchy, description of the problems he faced in Lisa's case. He also came clean and told Rosie about the dire legal consequences, for both himself and Quigley, if the case was lost. Rosie seemed to empathize, especially when it dawned on him that his prized young trial attorney and his closest associate would likely be disbarred if they lost Lisa's case. He knew Judge Taylor's terrible reputation for chewing up and devouring plaintiffs' attorneys and destroying their cases in the courtroom. Rosie had some choice words for Sean's opposition: "Those bastards at Howe and

Gates. I can't stand that wily, devious, untrustworthy Chauncy Howe. I can't believe how corrupt the healthcare system has become. The medical and insurance establishment defend bad medicine out of greed! I can't believe those money-hungry, two-faced medical experts, willing to lie to protect a bad doctor just to line their own pockets!"

Rosie was on a roll, and Sean was amused, considering the source. Rosie went on ranting: "I've never seen a bad medical case or a bad doctor that was not defended in court zealously and vigorously by the medical establishment and some of the most prominent doctors in this state." Rosie muttered how he hated the cancerous medical community using pressure tactics to bar plaintiffs from engaging medical experts.

As for Judge Taylor, Rosie fumed, "Taylor's an asshole who destroys every plaintiff's case he touches. He's no good. Never should have been a trial judge. He's caused so much harm and he's a disgrace to the judiciary. In fact, he's practically senile and mentally retarded to boot! With his high blood pressure and other physical problems, he should not be sitting as a judge." Rosie's parting shot as Sean stepped onto the elevator: "Good luck. Give 'em hell, Sean!"

Sean found this little pep talk comforting. He knew everything Rosie said was true and the commentary and encouraging words were welcome. "Rosie does have his moments," Sean thought.

As he left the building, he tried to steel himself for the upcoming court struggle. He chuckled to himself about some of Howe and Gates' outrageous pre-trial motions: to exclude Lisa from sitting with her parents because it could evoke unnecessary and needless sympathy; to exclude Lisa from the courtroom during the entire trial as that could evoke unnecessary sympathy; to exclude her from entering the court until her day of testimony as that could unfairly affect the jury. Another Motion was to exclude any juror who ever had a medical disease or heath problems which meant that there would probably be no juror that would ever able be to sit on the case.

Sean knew that jury selection was of critical importance. Unless he picked the right jury, no matter how skillfully he prepared the case or examined the defense at trial, he would not be able to win the case. His case would be in their hands. He hoped and prayed that he would choose wisely.

The impending case was no longer just a case but the final battle. This would be Sean's last legal battle, his last case. To lose would be a terrible blow for Lisa and for him. The stakes were mounting, like a poker game gone wild. Someone would lose big.

Chapter 11

Peer Pressure

The next day, Sean, sensing mounting pressure of the upcoming trial, left his office early and took a long walk along the waterfront for much-needed diversion and mental relaxation. He enjoyed the tranquility of his waterfront strolls and used these moments to refresh his spirit and to recharge his depleted batteries. His mind, saturated with Lisa's case and with doubts about its outcome, tossed and turned like a jumpy washing machine. He went over his tactics and strategies again and again.

As for life after the case, Sean's thoughts fixated on one idea: "If I am successful, this could truly be my last case." Trial work, he now realized, had become too stressful, too hostile, too matter of life or death. He wondered how much pressure any one lawyer could handle in his lifetime and how much he could endure until he mentally and physically collapsed. Lisa's case would be his "last hurrah," his last medical trial.

As he walked, his mind slowly relaxed. Sean loved these waterfront excursions. He focused on the glimmering rays of sunshine reflected off the ever-changing hues of the harbor waters. He was enchanted by the changing harbor scenes, ships and commuter boats, a sailboat here and an incoming airplane there, car freighters, cruise ships. The harbor never slept.

Sean used the harbor images as his form of escape. He dreamt of boats and far away places. It was, for him, a form of meditation that refreshed and invigorated both body and soul. He always felt years younger and happy after these harbor jaunts.

Instead of rushing back to the battlefield, Sean wandered into the Faneuil Hall Marketplace and had lunch at an outside table at the Salty Dog where he could sit and watch the dizzying array of tourists parading before him. He enjoyed this late afternoon repast and felt as if he were a tourist on a Roman holiday himself. Sean lingered at his table an hour or so after. When he finally returned to his office, he felt rested and ready to take on the most challenging case of his career.

This near euphoria changed the instant he saw his telephone messages. Dr. Grouper had called and his call was starred URGENT. The very word sent Sean's heart pounding. Dr. Grouper, chief of nephrology at Pediatric Hospital, was Dr. Hamilton's boss. The note said, "Must speak to you today. Please call."

The message terrified Sean. It could mean a storm was brewing on the horizon, and at this late date, any potential problem could be fatal to Lisa's case. Sean was already stretched as far as he could go. There was no time or energy left for any slip-ups, mistakes, or even disappointments.

Sean trembled as he dialed the number and, after several transfers, Dr. Grouper came on the line. In a rather stern, authoritative and commanding voice, Dr. Grouper stated he wanted to meet with Sean to discuss Dr. Hamilton's direct involvement as a medical expert at trial. Dr. Grouper explained to Sean that he had been on the telephone with the president of Pediatric's Board of Trustees. "He told me in no uncertain terms that it is the hospital policy at Pediatric Hospital not to allow junior doctors to testify in court on a medical malpractice case without the direct approval of their medical chief. Testifying in court disrupts the operating and surgical schedules of junior doctors at teaching hospitals, such as Dr. Hamilton. Only in exceptionally compelling cases should Pediatrics ever consider allowing any doctor to testify in Court." Sean's heart stopped as he heard these remarks. He was barely able to think. His mind went totally blank. He knew he would lose the case if Dr. Hamilton was not able to testify in court. He needed Dr. Hamilton's expert testimony at trial to have any hope of winning a jury verdict. "Dr.

Grouper," Sean pleaded, "Give me a few minutes to meet with you. Can I come right over?"

"It's now 4:00 P.M. I'll see you at in half an hour." The line went silent.

Sean was in a total frenzy and frantically hailed a cab. Pediatrics was, fortunately, only a fifteen-minute cab ride away but Sean was applying Murphy's law and dreaded the worse. If he lost Dr. Hamilton as a medical expert, his case was doomed.

Dr. Grouper greeted Sean coolly but politely and thanked him for coming over on such short notice. He explained that he had just been contacted about the case by the hospital president and several of the hospital's most powerful and influential Trustees. Grouper was also contacted that day by Dr. Richard Stern, the chief of pediatrics at neighboring Tremont Hospital, another teaching hospital. Dr. Stern had told him in no uncertain terms that Tremont had invoked its long-standing policy not to allow junior doctors to testify in medical malpractice cases. He had specifically ordered Dr. O'Reilly not to testify in Lisa's case. Dr. Stern now was simply checking with me to see if Pediatrics would invoke the same rigid policy that was in conformity with all the teaching hospitals in the Boston area." After Sean heard this comment, he was shocked. He suddenly, in one felt swoop, had lost Dr. O'Reilly, his one and only pediatric

witness, and was now on the verge of losing Dr.
Hamilton, his one and only kidney specialist.
Would he now lose his last hope, his last medical
expert, Dr. Hamilton? Lisa was now on the verge
of losing her case because her case required medical
experts and she could not try her case without
medical experts such as Dr. Hamilton supporting
her case.

Sean knew immediately that the insidious
and evil forces of Howe and Gates had reached out
their tentacles and were working behind the scenes.
Chauncy Howe had wasted no time contacting the
chief of pediatrics at Tremont through third parties
to prohibit O'Reilly from testifying as Sean's
witness. Attorney Howe was cleverly creating the
necessary roadblocks to destroy Sean's case. If
Howe and Gates could succeed in eliminating all of
Sean's medical experts, Lisa would be defenseless.
Sean would have no medical experts at trial and
could not present his case to a jury. Lisa's case
would have to be dismissed.

Chauncy Howe was clearly ahead in the
legal chess game. He was using his extensive
medical contacts and the powerful Boston medical
establishment to prevent Lisa from having any
medical support at trial and to simply destroy her
case. To Sean's way of thinking, Howe's dirty,
sneaky tricks bordered on criminal and unethical

conduct. Howe was applying peer-pressure tactics to intimidate Sean's medical experts to quit the case and with great success. This conduct was contemptible and outrageous, but how would Sean be able to prove this in a court of law? Chauncy Howe had evidently pushed the right buttons at both Tremont and Pediatric, but he did it so discretely and carefully, through third or fourth parties, that Howe and Gates' dirty hands and powerful influence could never be traced directly back to them.

It is certainly considered unethical, and for that matter, criminal conduct for an attorney to deliberately threaten a witness and Sean knew that this tactic of interfering with medical witnesses was totally unethical and illegal. But it was only one of a number of dirty tricks sometimes used by the medical insurers to win medical cases. Sean's mind raced back to earlier days when he recalled the time he was representing an uninsured doctor as a defendant in a medical malpractice case and was his personal defense attorney. While defending him, he became aware that certain medical records in the case had suddenly become "unavailable". Sean learned from other defense attorneys that the necessary records had somehow been "misplaced" or "misfiled". He could never understand what had happened to these critical records and what active part the insurance carrier or the defense attorneys played in their sudden disappearances? Sean mused, "If the public only knew the extent of the underhanded measures used by insurers to win cases at the expense of total integrity." Again, Sean thought did the end justify the means? No. But this is how medical cases were tried and it sickened him. What had become of justice and truth?

But Sean's Waterloo loomed before him; the critical moment had arrived. In one moment, one conversation, he had not only lost one critical expert, Dr. O'Reilly, but now was about to lose his second critical expert, Dr. Hamilton. In order to save Hamilton from being dismissed, Sean would have to be at his best and most eloquent. Now with everything to lose, Sean spoke from his heart with every ounce of integrity and sincerity in his body. This was his moment of truth:

"Dr. Grouper, this court case is not about Pediatrics, Tremont or the medical establishment. It's about a little girl who has suffered the worst medical negligence possible. This case is about Lisa and about the principle that good medical care would have saved both of her kidneys while bad care destroyed both of them. This case is about how bad medicine has now placed Lisa's life in serious jeopardy. The time has come for someone to stand up for Lisa against bad medicine and the terribly mismanaged medical case. Dr. Hamilton is willing to do so, and so am I. On behalf of Lisa, as her lawyer, I'm asking you," he paused, "I'm literally begging you, Doctor, to give Dr. Hamilton that opportunity. Lisa needs your help and she desperately needs Dr. Hamilton's help at this moment. Please allow Dr. Hamilton to testify at trial on Lisa's behalf."

Sean watched the doctor's face and demeanor. Grouper's face remained expressionless. Sean couldn't tell if his final pleas had in any way moved him. The doctor stood erect without moving and then, with his hands behind his back, circled his desk several times. He looked out his window for several moments, seeming to be lost in thought. Suddenly, he picked up the phone and paged Dr. Hamilton to come to his office immediately. Sean's hopes faded. "This is not a good sign," he thought.

Lisa's case looked dead in the water. He thought that Dr. Grouper was about to read the riot act and invoke the rigid hospital policy doctor Stein had done at Tremont to prohibit Dr. O'Reilly from testifying. Sean's worse fears were being realized. The end was in sight both for Lisa and for his legal career. All he could do was to try to look composed and casual. Of course, this was a total bluff. His body was trembling and he knew that if he tried to speak, his voice would crack.

Dr. Grouper glanced at Sean, who was obviously downtrodden, as Dr. Hamilton cruised casually into the office. "How's everything, Bill?" Dr. Grouper said. "You've already met Sean. He speaks very highly of you and is very grateful for your cooperation and assistance. I told Sean about our inflexible and somewhat rigid policy of not allowing junior physicians to testify in court on medical cases unless there is approval from their chief and an exceptionally compelling reason to do so. Generally, since I have been chief, I haven't allowed junior doctors to testify as experts in medical cases. Court engagements and testimony disrupts the surgical and clinical work of our department, which you know is already understaffed, and places the overall care of our patients at risk."

Sean held his breath. He felt the ax was about to fall. But Dr. Grouper''s face suddenly changed and he became very emotional and animated. "You know, Bill, I've gone to a lot of medical meetings and seminars over the last thirty years. Recently, at these professional events, spokespeople for the insurance industry and the Boston medical defense establishment, led particularly by Howe and Gates, have been lecturing doctors and hospital personnel and warning us not to get involved testifying in court for plaintiffs and injured patients on medical malpractice cases. The prohibitive message always troubled me. It is threatening, intimidating and borders on peer pressure. To me, to honor their prohibition message means protecting bad medicine by protecting doctors, regardless of their level of competence and the terrible injury they can cause innocent patients."

"I find this prohibition policy about testifying extremely distasteful and very upsetting. I've always believed that bad medicine should be rooted out and corrected, and good medicine protected and defended. Doctors practicing good medicine within the standard of care should move to eliminate bad medicine and zealously speak out against the bad. Otherwise, the system will never change. Bill, you and I represent Pediatrics, one of the most highly rated teaching hospitals in Massachusetts, in the country and, for that matter, in the world. Through our medical careers, we must take a stand to protect the quality of medical care and do everything within our power to prevent and eliminate bad medicine. I've looked at Lisa's case and it upsets me terribly. I have repeatedly advised our pediatric referrals that the dip stick method for testing is totally unreliable for detecting long-term kidney infections. My words, however, have fallen on deaf ears. I know many doctors now make a

huge profit performing these antiquated tests, even
when more accurate and more precise tests are
available at any hospital in Massachusetts.
Urinalysis is the gold standard and, as you know, is
the most accurate and precise test for testing protein
in the urine, not dip sticks.

I have been sickened and shocked to see
pediatric kidney infection referrals increasing from
year to year because of these unreliable dip stick
studies. I never thought I would be saying this but I
believe now is the time for our hospital to take a
stand against this substandard practice.

Within a year, I had planned to resign as
chief. You would then step in as chief of this
department, Bill. However, now you're in for a
battlefield promotion today. In Sean's presence, I
hereby appoint you Acting Chief of the Nephrology
Department of Pediatrics Hospital. Thus, if you
decide, which I hope you do, to testify in court on
Lisa's behalf, you no longer need my approval as
your chief. Personally, I believe you should testify.
You know the intricacies of Lisa's kidney disease.
You are her treating doctor and are uniquely
qualified to explain to a lay jury all the aspects of
her kidney complications, and to describe the lack
of proper care she received at the hands of her
treating pediatricians. And, Bill, in the future,
don't you think we should change this dumb policy

not allowing junior doctors to testify in Court? Don't you agree this is a destructive rather than constructive policy?" Dr. Hamilton responded, "Of course I do. I can tell you from this day forward that policy is no longer in effect. I know we'll get some heat from the president and trustees but, that will blow over. As you know, even their policy indicated it could be done under an exceptional situation and I do find these circumstances involving Lisa very exceptional."

Sean could not believe what he had heard and what was transpiring between Dr. Grouper and Dr. Hamilton. Suddenly, his darkest moment was brightened and he was happier than he had ever been since he had been involved in the case. Who could have foreseen this dramatic turn of events? Sean looked at Dr. Hamilton whose beaming smile and gratitude spoke volumes. You could see in Dr. Hamilton's face and demeanor a determination to testify on Lisa's behalf. Sean vigorously shook Grouper's hand and told him how much he admired his great courage. He told him he certainly made a great appointment and that Dr. Hamilton would make a wonderful chief.

Chapter 12

The Opening Salvo

The fatal day had arrived. The jury had been picked. There was an air of anticipation in the courtroom. The trial was to begin. Both attorneys were in deep thought. Sean was bracing himself to make his opening statement to the jury.

Sean started to speak. However, before a word reached his lips, Judge Taylor rudely interrupted. This was a well-known Taylor tactic designed to upset Sean and throw off his opening and his sense of timing. Taylor loudly screamed for Sean to approach side bar. Taylor was short-tempered and redder than ever. Judge Taylor's high blood pressure was evidently acting up and, evidently, his pain medication was not having a positive effect on him. "Mr. McArthur," he said in an angry tone, "I expect you to have your list of witnesses on my desk by 9 A.M. tomorrow. Do you get my drift? By the way, thank you Attorney Howe for following my rule of court and for presenting your list of witnesses to me several weeks in advance. I appreciate that very much." Then Taylor shot another angry look at Sean and, in a loud voice, further conducted his lecture: "Mr. McArthur, in the future when you try cases before me, I expect you to have your list of witnesses a week before trial." Sean attempted to use every meditation technique at his disposal to remain calm and cool and was attempting to act as though this scolding did not hurt him. But, inside he knew it did. All the time while Judge Taylor persisted in his harangue, Sean was losing points with the jury. Sean recognized this outburst as an effort to upset him and he tried not to rise to the bait. He knew what he had to do in his opening to the jury and he believed he could do it, even though he knew the odds were great. He felt more determined than ever to put in a great case. Many court experts know that many a case is lost or won on the opening to the jury. First impressions do mean a lot especially at trial.

Sean proceeded to make his opening statement and slowly ambled to the front of the jury. He felt for the first time in a long time strangely at ease. He earnestly looked each of the fourteen jurors in the eye and began to softly speak, almost in a whisper so the jury had to strain to hear what he was saying, "Lisa Rowe is a beautiful young thirteen year old girl. Her life is now in jeopardy a result of the terrible neglect inflicted upon her over a six-year span of time by her own treating doctors whom she trusted so much." Sean knew that these first words to the jury were probably the most important words he would speak in the trial. He knew the words should not be intimidating or angry but should be clear and precise and succinctly and simply state the medical essence of Lisa's case. Sean looked again at each juror with eye contact as he knew each of them individually had the fate of his client in their hands and he was sincerely appealing to them to be fair, open-minded, and impartial in reviewing Lisa's case.

Sean continued in a very smooth manner still maintaining intense eye contact with the jury, "I have the privilege to represent a young, vulnerable girl whose kidneys were totally destroyed, not by any fault of hers but because of errors and neglect committed by her treating doctors. It's hard to believe that over a period of six-years, medical mistakes were made by her doctors who were caring for Lisa. You will hear how tragic errors and mistakes were committed by Dr. Smith, Dr. Blade and by Savin Medical. These critical mistakes and errors resulted in Lisa losing one kidney and now being in danger of losing the other. You will hear how the total failure of her own treating doctors, whom she trusted so much to perform appropriate lab tests and follow up on urine tests, did not do what they were supposed to do and failed to promptly refer her to an expert urologist or to a treating hospital over a six year period of time.

This was a drastic error and a terrible mistake on their part. You will hear how this drastic error and terrible mistake had devastating medical consequences and how this error and mistake destroyed Lisa's life and severely diminished her life expectancy. You will see the medical records and these records will support a case against her physicians." As Sean uttered these words, internally he was saying a prayer to himself. He had no right making that statement about the medical records as he himself hadn't seen all of Lisa's medical records and he was assuming that the records would be helpful. He was taking a gamble mentioning the records as supporting her case in his opening statement. This was a dangerous gamble but, under the circumstances, Sean thought he had no choice. In order to favorably present Lisa's case to the jury, he was willing to take this risk.

Sean, as he was concluding, glanced at his watch – one minute remained of the fifteen. He could see from the corner of his eye that Judge Taylor was growing restless. Sean knew he had to finish quickly or he would be chastised by an ill-tempered judge. He quickly concluded and was in the process of thanking the jury for their attention when, suddenly, Judge Taylor rudely interrupted, "Mr. McArthur, your time has expired". Sean was flabbergasted by this unnecessary interruption as it was clear that he was a minute under his fifteen minutes of time and was concluding his opening statement when the rude interruption occurred. Sean, with a polite nod to the jury, returned to counsel table relieved and pleased that his opening had been completed. He thought the opening, even with the short period of time, was interesting. He discussed several of the medical components and, hopefully, captured the interest and intellectual curiosity of the jury. He could tell by how intensely the jury was following his words and how they were looking at him afterwards that they were interested in hearing further evidence regarding the medical issues he was discussing. For the first time that day, Sean felt the tension empty from his body. He felt nearly euphoric. However, this would be a momentary feeling. He knew it would change and it did as Attorney Howe walked over and now stood before the jury.

Sean knew that Howe was a formidable trial attorney. He was very egocentric and often bragged to his cronies at the Harvard Club and at the defense bar meetings that he had never lost a medical case in thirty years. He was successful because his trial strategy was simply to psychologically impose his will on the opposing counsel and win favor with the jury. He was a true pro – very experienced.

Howe, exuding confidence, addressed the jury with the air of a polished professional. His ruddy face, intense blue eyes, and imposing six foot one stature commanded attention and were a definite asset. Howe looked seasoned, very much like one of the many celebrated physicians he had successfully defended throughout his trial career. He warmly smiled at the jury and they reciprocated. Howe presented a comfortable and commanding presence and inspired trust. One could see he was no stranger to the courtroom. The courtroom was his stage and he enjoyed being a star performer.

Howe immediately identified his clients as dedicated and outstanding pediatricians, pillars of the medical community. He emphasized that both doctors were leading pediatricians and recognized nationally and internationally for their accomplishments. Howe even praised Savin Medical, stating it was "the most highly recognized and largest medical HMO in Massachusetts, it had the highest level of quality care and only engaged doctors who were board certified in their area of specialty and had been peer reviewed by their colleagues. He emphasized how, year in and year out, Savin Medical had won national awards as one of the top HMOs in the country, and that they had been featured on television and in TIME magazine as an outstanding HMO. He was making the best use of his allotted fifteen minutes.

Most defense attorneys enjoy spending quality time in front of the jury rebutting and challenging the plaintiff's case. It gives seasoned defense counsel a great opportunity to challenge every statement made by the plaintiff without worrying about an immediate rebuttal by plaintiff's counsel. The object for the defense in its opening statement is to create doubts in the minds of the jury about the credibility of the plaintiff's case. Chauncy Howe was a master at this. Quickly and quietly he effectively raised doubts about Lisa's case. Everywhere he could, he poked holes in Sean's opening statement: It was medically unsound; Drs. Smith and Blade had not done anything wrong but, in fact, had provided exemplary care, well above the professional standard. Howe emphasized that the appropriate test and procedures were done and were completely in accordance with the standard of care. He quietly emphasized how dedicated the doctors were to Lisa and that she had received not merely good care, but exceptional medical care.

Sean could tell at a glance that the jury was listening intently to Attorney Howe and that he definitely had their attention and support. Howe was using a familiar defendant's tactic. He lined up top medical experts, pitting their superior qualifications, superior academic backgrounds, and their superior clinical experience against the plaintiff's experts. Howe put it to the jury bluntly: "Do you really believe that these outstanding and highly respected physicians would come here, to this courtroom, from all over the country and testify under oath on behalf of the defendants if they had any doubts about their skill and competence?"

He gestured toward Drs. Smith and Blade, identifying them for the jury, and they turned their heads to the spectator section where the doctors sat with their glamorous but very respectable wives. Sean noted with alarm that a number of the jurors smiled warmly and nodded to the doctors. His sense of alarm increased when he saw who was sitting right beside Dr. Smith. It was Bishop Robert Clarkson, an Episcopalian, who was a very active community advocate. He worked with the homeless and he was well known and admired in Massachusetts. It seemed to Sean that whatever positive effect his persuasive opening had made, it was fading fast. Some members of the jury glanced at him quizzically.

Juries have a thousand eyes and miss very little of what happens in the courtroom. Sean could not help but think that the church, in the form of Bishop Robert Clarkson, was well-represented and was present to anoint the defendants' case – not to bless the plaintiff's. He also knew that the jury would be well-acquainted with the impressive educational, social, and community works of the defendants' wives, both of whom were active in various charitable works in Massachusetts, and particularly in the Boston area. Over the years they had often been featured on the society pages of the Boston Globe and the Boston Herald.

Sean realized, too, that in cases like these, defendants have an edge. Juries are always impressed when they hear the professional qualifications of the medical defendants. The defendants have an additional psychological advantage: Each jury member had likely had to rely upon doctors to stay well and therefore would be reluctant to think that any doctor could do wrong. The jury certainly would give the doctors the benefit of the doubt.

Attorney Howe spoke impressively for twenty-two minutes, seven minutes over the allotted time. Judge Taylor was definitely employing a double standard at this trial, allowing defense counsel a more generous time limitation than plaintiff's counsel. Howe's seven additional minutes had scored critical points.

With the cards stacked against him, Sean fidgeted in his chair, looked at his watch, glanced at the jury, and kept shaking his head. He hoped that his body language and apparent distress would send a message to the jury that the playing field was lopsided and unfair. He wanted the jury to recognize that Lisa's case was already being extremely prejudiced by a biased pro-defense judge.

Chauncy Howe spoke to the jury in a smooth clear manner. He was learned and very well-informed, sounding like a doctor presenting a medical case. When he finally finished his opening, Sean could tell that the jury was impressed with Howe's extensive knowledge. He had described the confusing medical terms and made the case sound very complex but, because of his obvious grasp of the details, he also showed that he knew Lisa's case inside out. The jury had to be impressed with his performance.

Even Sean was impressed with the depth and clarity of Howe's presentation. He recognized how Howe's strategy was paying dividends and that he was definitely winning favor with the jury. While Sean had tried to make Lisa's case simple and understandable, Attorney Howe was emphasizing its complexities, making the case seem mysterious. The effect was to imply that there were legitimate reasons why the defendants treated Lisa as they did, and how the medical nuances he discussed were consistent with their decisions.

When Howe finished, Sean breathed a sigh of relief and muttered to himself, "I'm glad that's over." The first day before the jury was at an end. At that moment, Judge Taylor tossed yet another curve ball. He rose quickly, but he did not leave the bench. To Sean's surprise, Taylor addressed the jury: "You've heard both openings. I want you to keep an open mind in the case and I'm also telling you the plaintiff always has the burden of proof. The plaintiff's burden of proof means the plaintiff must present credible medical evidence to you and must prove this case by the preponderance of the evidence. Preponderance of evidence is a **tremendous** and **heavy burden** on the plaintiff.

"You may, during the trial, see me have side bar conferences with counsel. These conferences ensure that no improper evidence is introduced by overly aggressive counsel. You may see me react sometimes at the bench. If I do, it is because I am trying to keep out evidence that should not be before you. I also will instruct you when I object to a question and exclude it. When this happens, you should disregard the question and when I object to an answer and exclude it, you must disregard the answer as well. I will continue to instruct you as the case progresses. I look forward to seeing you first thing at 9 A.M. sharp tomorrow morning." With that, he abruptly left the courtroom.

Sean was stunned and sat immobile. He recognized that Judge Taylor was doing everything he possibly could to influence a case favorable to the defendant. This so-called "impartial" judge had not even instructed the jurors not to discuss the case among themselves, with anyone else, or pay attention to the newspaper, TV, or other media. It seemed likely, with these sloppy instructions, that the jury would spend the first night talking about it with family members and some would probably read or hear about it in the media. Sean knew he was well on his way to losing the case before even introducing a witness.

Sean sat in a state of shock and watched the courtroom slowly empty out. He felt lonely and defeated. His dream of making the first day a success had disintegrated and it now looked like his chances of winning the case would be impossible. He imagined the same jury he addressed today, filing in a week later with a verdict in favor of the defendants. At this point he felt there was very little he could do. Judge Taylor knew that Sean did not have the medical records and the judge would make it difficult for Sean to obtain them. He wanted to cry, but tears would do no good. He had to collect and organize his thoughts and then ride the exploding waves of the day-to-day litigation.

Each day would bring new surprises, new shocks. Battles would be lost but the war must be won.

Cases are usually won on the first or the last day of the trial. In a medical case especially, losing the opening day's activities is considered a bad omen and the kiss of death, as most plaintiff's attorneys who win do so on their opening. Sean sensed that his opening, although extremely effective, was not as effective as Chauncy Howe's. Defendants' counsel had effectively rebutted and then claimed the high ground with the quality of his medical testimony and on the quality of his expert witnesses. Round 1 belonged to Chauncy Howe.

Sean surveyed the courtroom and it was empty except for Ed Sheridan, who was heading his way. "Sean, I think you've got a tiger by the tail here," Sheridan said. "Taylor can be tough. He doesn't like plaintiffs, but don't let that get under your skin. Don't lose your cool. Stay with it. Tomorrow's another day." Sean thanked Ed for his encouraging words and thought: "Maybe there is some hope. All is not lost. It's a day-to-day battle. Maybe the tide will turn." And he **was** happy about one thing – he had not been humiliated by Attorney Howe moving for a dismissal. Sean had known enough about the case to present a prima facie case in the opening.

Leaving court, Sean stopped by the Clerk's office to see if the medical records that he had summonsed had arrived. The records weren't in yet, even though the case was underway. The records, Sean knew, probably would not be available to him until he presented witnesses. Howe definitely did not want to give Sean the benefit of reviewing the records before he had the defendants on the witness stand. It would make a tougher course for Sean to present a meaningful cross-examination of any of the defendant doctors.

He drove back to his office in a daze. All he could think about was the case – it was all consuming. Everyone in the office knew that when he was at trial, he acted like a zombie. They were reluctant to talk to him because he seemed to be in a totally different world. Sean leafed through the pile of telephone messages on the desk, the usual array from client and referring attorneys. He made it a point when he was on a trial not to return calls unless they pertained directly to the case. He could not give in to any distractions. He noted that his secretary had made yet another call to Attorney Howe to try to obtain all of the medical records, but it was unsuccessful. He knew it would be.

Sean's thoughts turned to his first witness. He knew that either of Lisa's parents would make a poor witness. Neither had a clear memory of the doctor visits and the only way they could identify particular appointments would be by telephone messages and bills. Sean could see Attorney Howe having a field day with Mrs. Rowe. She was confused to begin with and never seemed to be certain on any particular issue. She would be easily trapped and questioned and would not make a good appearance on the substantive part of the case. Mr. Rowe was an engineer and wanted to be as precise as possible. But, this would be his downfall. He never went along with his wife when Lisa was examined by the defendants. He only played "Monday morning quarterback," and just questioned his wife as to why his daughter was sick. In fact, he knew very little about Lisa's case and her treatment.

This was a problem. Sean knew he had to have a strong first witness to present to the jury, someone who would be articulate, dramatic, and very impressive. He thought about several cases he had tried in the past in which he started off with a witness he thought would be the strongest only to have that witness collapse on the stand and cost him the case. On close cases you're not entitled to any mistakes. Sean couldn't risk this happening this time. Whomever Sean selected had to make a good first impression in order to sustain jury interest throughout the trial. Who could he pick who would be able to withstand the onslaught of a precise and slashing cross-examination by one of the best defense counsels in the state?

He glanced again at the messages on the Rowe case. Several of Lisa's teachers had returned his calls. He would get back to them right away.

Chapter 13

The First Witness

The night before, Sean had agonized about trial strategy. Presenting witnesses is the most critical part of a trial. Juries are notorious for being creatures of first impression and Sean's first witness had to be someone dynamic who would immediately win their sympathy. He considered putting on one of the defendants, Dr. Smith or Dr. Blade, the head of Savin Medical, but this was very dangerous. It is very important to launch the plaintiff's case with a witness the jury can understand. Sean was afraid that, even though he knew a great deal medically and anatomically about kidneys, the jury wouldn't have equal knowledge and therefore would not be able to follow his examination of the defendants. And, he still didn't have the critical medical records he needed. Without these records he could not conduct an effective cross-examination of either Dr. Smith or Dr. Blade.

With his head reeling with strategy and tactics, Sean drove to the courthouse, a half-hour from his home. "This is a no-brainer," he thought. "The only witness I can call, and the most dynamic and important one, would be Lisa!" Lisa Rowe, thirteen years old, was young and vulnerable. She would make a definite favorable impression on the jury and, he hoped, evoke sympathy because her medical problems were life-threatening.

How could any juror dislike a beautiful, fragile, loveable thirteen-year-old who was on the brink of losing both kidneys, and would likely be on dialysis for the rest of her life and therefore subject to severe infections that could lead to premature death. Lisa did not have to be a good historian when she described her sickness and visits to doctors over a six-year period. The jury would have to be heartless to doubt her and to ignore the fact that she was very sick and not getting better despite her best efforts. After reviewing his options one more time, he knew he had made the right choice. Lisa Rowe would be his first witness.

It was Sean's practice to meet with his potential witnesses an hour before trial for a final briefing. In the past Sean often spent time in the office with his witnesses the day before trial and even called them at home to review the details of the case. The time spent the hour before trial, however, was the most meaningful and significant and would be the most critical time that Sean and Lisa's witnesses would spend together because they would be at their most alert and Sean had to be at his best.

At the courthouse Sean met briefly with Mr. and Mrs. Rowe and told them that Lisa would be his first witness. He then spoke to Lisa. They had become good friends: Lisa seemed to enjoy Sean's casual sense of humor; Sean was always ready to make her laugh when she came to his office. She constantly questioned him about the origins of the various artifacts he collected and displayed in his office: a brass alligator, a replica of Air Force Two, Indian artifacts, a stealth bomber, wood carvings, a rock in the shape of an owl, and all sorts of strange exotic items. He enjoyed kidding with Lisa and they had established a wonderful and close relationship within a short time. He could tell that she trusted him and had confidence in him. Sean had observed that Lisa was intelligent, sensitive, and seemed to have amazing recall of her terrible nightmare over the last six years.

Sean politely asked her parents if he could spend some private time with Lisa. The parents concurred, so Sean and Lisa proceeded down the corridor to a small private conference room. They sat down and Sean casually began to crack a few jokes. He spent the first fifteen minutes just talking with Lisa, as if they were having another friendly chat in the office. He did not want to unduly alarm her at this time, although every one of his nerve endings reminded him that the entire case might hinge on Lisa's testimony. Sean glanced at his watch and realized time was growing short. He had only forty-five minutes to prepare Lisa, his most important witness. If she did not do well on the stand, the case would not go well at all.

Sean gradually switched from small talk to more serious matters about Lisa and her kidney problem. He told her that he would present her to the jury this morning and that she should be herself and the jury would like her. "They want to hear all the details about your case," Sean told her. "The jury will be listening to you very carefully and will want to know what happened to you." He went on to explain that the jury would especially want to hear how her teachers had been so good to her and how she had developed a very special love for them.

Lisa lit up and smiled warmly when Sean told her she would now have a chance to tell how so many people had helped her get through her days of painful illness. "Each juror will be looking at you and you should look them right in the eye and tell them what happened," he said. Sean cautioned Lisa about Judge Taylor: "Sometimes he interrupts and he might seem stern, but that is his job. Don't be concerned about that." Sean wanted to make sure she was psychologically capable of dealing with any interruptions that occurred in the courtroom.

Sean also told Lisa that the defense attorney might also suddenly interrupt and object to something they were saying. "But," Sean explained, "even though you may think it's rude, that's his job and I don't want you to be concerned with that." The most important thing in the courtroom was to just tell the truth about what happened and tell everything that she could remember. Sean told her he would tell the jury about her sickness and the days she missed from school. He asked her to try to remember any conversations she may have had with Dr. Smith or Dr. Blade, particularly if they told her not to worry and that they would take good care of her. "I want you to tell the jury, just like you've told me before when we talked in my office, how you believed Dr. Smith and Dr. Blade were helping you to get better." Sean thought it was important that the jury hear the story in Lisa's own words and not to have her testimony sound prompted, rehearsed, or scripted. After thirty minutes he wrapped up their conversation and walked with her back down the corridor to her mother and father. He wanted her to have some breathing room to relax and to be herself before she testified. He did not want her racing from the conference room into the courtroom. That would be too nerve wracking.

This would be the first time the jury would observe Lisa. As a tactical matter, and to add some measure of suspense and excitement, Sean had deliberately excluded Lisa during the first day of opening statements. He thought it would be more effective to present Lisa to the jury suddenly and unexpectedly in order to create interest. Sean wanted to direct, choreograph, and introduce his witness in the most interesting and meaningful fashion so the case would flow easily and the jury would retain its interest and curiosity. Sean thought of lawyers as producers of great dramas, in control of production and direction. At a few minutes before 9:00, he ushered his actors into the courtroom, and onto the stage.

Promptly at 9:00 A.M, the swinging doors that led to chambers flew open with a banging so loud it could be heard throughout the courthouse. Judge Taylor crashed through and marched over to the bench. His face was redder than ever and his temper seemed worse than the day before, if that were possible.

He slammed his ever-present black notebook onto the table, emitting a frightening loud noise, the first barrage of the day's artillery that sent swords and daggers throughout Sean's body. Taylor angrily struck his gavel onto the bench and barked out in his piercing, raspy voice, "Court is now in session!"

Sean bit his lip, closed his eyes, meditated for a brief moment, and said a silent prayer. He just hoped that he could present Lisa's case without being derailed, destroyed, or torpedoed by Judge Taylor. For his own sense of confidence, Sean wanted to get off to a good start. The drama was building. Spectators waited in awe and eager anticipation for the staged battle to begin.

The fourteen citizens sitting in the jury box surveyed every inch of the courtroom. You could see by their eager expressions that they were looking forward to the day's proceedings. Jurors' interest is at its height at the beginning of the case. That is when you have their undivided attention. The previous day's opening statements had engaged this jury and they sensed that they were about to hear a significant and important medical case. They knew they had an important part in this drama and they were eager to play it.

Judge Taylor, dispensed with saying good morning to the jury and shouted out in a particularly grating tone, "Mr. McArthur! Present your first witnesses!" Most trial judges are polite to attorneys, especially at the outset of the trial. But Judge Taylor was not one to be polite or caring. He was abrupt and harsh by nature to plaintiffs and their attorneys. This was his modus operandi, his "style." In a calm controlled voice, Sean asked Lisa Rowe to take the stand. While she walked to the front, he looked over at Attorney Howe's coterie of lawyers and paralegals who were seated at the defense table, adjacent to the jury box. He wondered to himself how he had been outmaneuvered to allow the defense team to sit next to the jury. It bothered him, but he quickly brought his attention back to the task at hand.

Lisa had slowly gotten up from her high seat in the rear of the courtroom where she was ensconced between her parents and was walking with childlike dignity toward the front of the courtroom. She was escorted by a bulky six-foot court officer, probably a former longshoreman, who wore all the trappings of the court and who exuded authority and grandeur. The scene was bizarre. The contrast between the oversized court officer and tiny delicate Lisa was striking. She looked much younger than her thirteen years, a result of the kidney disease. She actually looked more like an eight-year-old. Sean could see that the jury was watching every step she took, and each step evoked some degree of sympathy. Some jurors already had tears in their eyes.

Sean observed that the courtroom seemed to contain a lot of white medical and nursing coats mixed throughout the spectator section. It was a well-known tactic used successfully by defense counsel in medical cases. They would fill the courtroom with medical personnel: young, energetic, attractive residents, fellows, and nurses, both male and female. The defense knew that their mere presence would support the defense and indirectly send a message to the jury. The odds against little Lisa were formidable.

Attorney Howe barely glanced at Lisa as she somehow managed to step up onto the witness stand, which was adult size and height. Sean was hoping that the jurors would notice Lisa's struggle just to get onto the stand. He also hoped they would take note of Howe's seeming hostility toward the child. Vigilant, conscientious, and sensitive jurors usually saw these things and took in the subtle body language and facial expressions of the parties in the courtroom. It all mattered when they sat down together in the jury room.

Judge Taylor lectured Lisa about being under oath and told her that she had to tell the truth. His voice was cold and unpleasant and Sean hoped the jurors were picking this up. Lisa bravely told the judge that she knew the difference between telling the truth and not telling the truth. She understood what a lie was. This small ceremony, which preceded her testimony, was very significant, thought Sean. It seemed to imprint on the jury that Lisa was there to tell the truth and that she understood that it was wrong not to tell the truth. He fervently hoped the jury would believe her.

Lisa looked small and fragile in the tall chair. She almost looked like a doll with her soft brown eyes and long brown hair. But the beauty of her eyes belied her physical weakness. Her complexion was sallow, and she was so thin that Sean could see the outline of her bones under her short-sleeved blue dress. Numerous bruises dotted both sides of her arms, and she had disfiguring scars around her wrists.

Slowly and deliberately, in a soft voice, Sean began his questions. The jury had to strain to hear. No one moved or made a sound in the courtroom. He spent the first fifteen minutes merely asking about Lisa's school activities, her hobbies, her interests, and her aspirations. The jurors leaned in intently and seemed to realize that Lisa, despite being a little girl, had great ambitions. She wanted to do well in school and was very unhappy because she was losing so much time from school, and from playing with her school friends, because of her sickness. Gradually, without being obvious, Sean wove into the case that Lisa frequently had been sick over a long period of time.

It had gotten to the point that she missed weeks at a time because of her illness.

Lisa told the court how her mother was required to help her with her homework, and how she always seemed to be behind. She was losing fifty school days each year and was recently told by one of her teachers that she might have to repeat a grade because she had missed so much. However, Lisa had worked hard and had managed to get caught up by attending summer school. She wanted to do well in school, she told them, because her dream was to be a doctor when she grew up.

Sean then began to question her in detail about her sickness. She described how she was urinating a great deal, how she frequently went to see her pediatrician, Dr. Smith, and how he was always kind to her. She told the jury how she trusted Dr. Smith and that she thought he was one of the best doctors in the world. She said that most of the time her mother took her to see the doctor and that she had been going for "years and years." She described how Dr. Smith did blood work and dip stick tests, and that he frequently took urine samples. Lisa told the jury that Dr. Smith always said she was "doing well" and how she did seem to get well after seeing him. She believed that he was the person who always made her feel better.

Sean asked her about her visits to Savin Medical for blood and urine studies, and for dip stick studies. She described how her mother would take her to see Dr. Blade at his clinic and that she would bring urine samples with her. He then asked her general questions about her six-year course of treatment, leaving out specific dates, which would be too much for a child to remember.

Throughout Lisa's testimony, Sean noticed that Judge Taylor glared at him, but never looked directly at Lisa or the jury. He also noticed that Chauncy Howe, now on his best behavior, smiled and never interrupted or raised an objection. Sean had hoped that Judge Taylor or Attorney Howe would interrupt because it might show the jury how biased and prejudiced Judge Taylor was as well as the true personality of Attorney Howe – obstructive and obnoxious. Sean thought of the old Irish expression, "World angels, house devils."

Lisa was doing well, Sean realized, but the defense was certainly not losing any points with the jury. He had planned on keeping her on the stand as long as possible without the risk of boring the jury, so he watched the mood closely. He asked a few questions about her treatment at Pediatric Hospital and how she was finally diagnosed. Then she described how different kidney tests were done which showed that she had already lost one kidney because it had shrunk from chronic long-term infection. The tests also showed that her other kidney had been 90 percent damaged by long-term infection. For a child, Lisa seemed to comprehend the medical jargon and terminology. She had become knowledgeable in many ways far beyond her years.

Sean intended to end her testimony on the most dramatic note possible. He had Lisa point to the wound on her wrist to show the jury where the nurse inserted the shunt that hooked her up to the dialysis machine. Lisa explained, in vivid detail, how the shunt, which was permanent, connected her to the machine three times a week. She said that she had to be on dialysis in order to live and that sometimes she had reactions to the treatment and would get very sick. Sean asked her about the numerous black and blue marks on both her arms and Lisa explained that they were from the many needles that were used over the years to take blood samples.

Sean decided that he would end his interrogation with a flourish: "What did you say you wanted to do when you grow up?" Lisa's responded simply, "I want to be a doctor, a pediatrician, and help sick children." Sean thanked her and, just as she seemed ready to leave the stand, Attorney Howe said politely, "Lisa, may I ask you a few questions?" Lisa looked up and, in a childlike manner, smiled radiantly. Her beautiful smile immediately softened her bruised and wounded physical appearance. "Yes," she answered quietly.

Attorney Howe merely asked whether Lisa liked Dr. Smith during the six years that he treated her, and asked her how the doctor treated her. She answered that he was always very friendly and very caring, although "sometimes he seemed to be in a hurry." Then Howe asked her the same questions about Dr. Blade and she said that he, too, also seemed to always be very busy but was "very nice." The cross-examination was friendly, bright, and concise – similar to Sean's direct. As Lisa concluded her testimony, the jurors seemed impressed with Lisa's condition, but did not seem upset at or to lose any good will towards Dr. Smith or Dr. Blade.

After Lisa's testimony, Judge Taylor asked counsel to approach the bench. Sean could see his hostility had not been lessened by Lisa's cheerful demeanor. Sean approached the bench, followed by Attorney Howe and his army of young attorneys. In a whispered tone, the jury wouldn't hear, he asked the Judge if the medical records he had summonsed had been filed in court. Sean wanted them introduced now as medical exhibits.

Judge Taylor looked over at Attorney Howe and asked, "Do you have any objection?" Howe stated that all of the relevant medical records were still in the possession of his clients, and Sean would be able to look at the originals only when they were introduced at trial when the doctors were on the stand. Howe asked the judge to rule that "Attorney McArthur not look at the records or have access to them until the witnesses are on the stand, as he had not sought them through discovery or by way of deposition prior to trial." Judge Taylor complied immediately and ruled, "Since plaintiff's counsel had not requested the records during pre-trial discovery, there is no need to have the medical records marked as trial exhibits now."

Judge Taylor suddenly veered out or control and began another tirade. His voice was loud enough for everyone to hear, particularly the jurors only fifteen feet away. "Mr. McArthur! I am disgusted by the way this case has been handled by your office and particularly by you. I'm not going to allow you to engage in this last minute desperate discovery tactic. This trial by ambush and sneaky last minute tactic is not one I approve of. I'm not going to allow you to look at the medical records until you call the defendants, and then I will give the defendants ample opportunity to review any record you suddenly submit to them.

"Mr. McArthur, now that you're at side bar, I want you to know I don't particularly like your underhanded tactics of introducing your first witness without identifying your order of witnesses to the court and opposing counsel. You know you should have identified your first witness to opposing counsel and to me. Professional courtesy, which you sorely lack, dictates that you do so. I insist that you identify for me and Attorney Howe every witness you intend to call. I want this on the day prior to their testifying so there are no surprises played upon defense counsel or the court. I detest your tactics and don't want any further surprises! Do you understand me? Do you get my drift? You got away with a fast one with your first witness but you're not going to get away with it any further in my court. Do you understand?"

Sean stood silent. He was astonished by this open vicious attack, but decided to just nod rather than to respond. He believed it was very important to be courteous at the bar and never to fight or argue with a trial judge. Anyway, judges always won. They had the last word. Judge Taylor, in a few scathing minutes, had negated the positive aspects of Lisa's testimony. Sean knew that the judge's explosion was deliberately calculated to weaken and destroy Sean's credibility and to tarnish his image before the jury. If this was his goal, Taylor seemed to be succeeding. Certain members of the jury stared at Sean with looks of disapproval.

The defense team clustered around Chauncy Howe, joking and kidding with one another. They acted very superior, confident, and casual. From their body language, Sean could tell that they felt very much in control and thought they were well on their way to winning the case.

As the jury filed out of the courtroom, some of them glanced at Sean with disapproval. Sean interpreted this as an ominous sign. The jury knew that he and Judge Taylor were not on the same wave-length and were hostile towards one another, and they were probably trying to figure out why Judge Taylor was so upset. Was Sean, in fact, a shady practitioner? Was he unethical and trying to pull a fast one on the court? The jury would certainly give Judge Taylor the benefit of the doubt. Sean knew that he was in for a miserable experience. He would have to do everything in his power to remain calm and not lose any more credibility with the jury. He hoped they would finally see Judge Taylor for the biased ass he truly was. Sean tried to think positively but the stress of the trial and Judge Taylor's constant barrages were psychologically disturbing him. His confidence was fading. He felt that he was losing control and his chance of winning jury confidence was quickly eroding. However, he knew that Dr. Hamilton would testify tomorrow and that buoyed his failing spirits. "There is still hope. Rome was not built in a day. There is always tomorrow."

Chapter 14

Day of Reckoning

The next day, Sean was flying high. He was so happy to see the cab deposit Dr. Hamilton curbside, and on schedule, that he tipped the driver twenty dollars. Dr. Hamilton's appearance at court was priceless. Without him, Sean could not hope to win the case, but now, Sean felt like the gods were shining on Lisa and him..

Sean knew this would be another critical day and he escorted Dr. Hamilton through the maze of mankind in the courtroom corridors and into the tiny conference room. The room was not modern by any means. It had a broken-down table and a few dilapitated chairs. However, it did offer some degree of privacy and seclusion to the attorneys and their clients.

Sean preferred to arrive at the courthouse early, as it was the first attorney who could grab one of the few conference rooms for a period of time and isolate his witnesses to prepare them for the trial. It was important to have the secrecy of a conference room versus the public exposure of courtroom corridors where other noisy, impulsive, and sometimes aggressive lawyers and their paralegal teams could overhear significant conversations. You could never have a private conversation in a corridor. The walls had a thousand ears.

Sean remembered the times he had spoken to his medical experts in the corridor. The defense counsel would hover about, trying to listen in. This was often accompanied by hostile, angry, and aggressive glares directed at his witnesses. This was the type of psychological warfare novice witnesses had to deal with upon entering the world of litigation. Warfare was already launched and tactics underway to intimidate a witness. Sean did not want to expose Dr. Hamilton to this type of grilling and intimidation, especially since he was inexperienced testifying in court.

As he walked the doctor to the conference room, Sean's mind raced. He was thinking of too many things at once and was desperately trying to keep his mind quiet and his body from jumping out of its skin. He knew that Ms. Murray, Lisa's teacher, would be arriving at 8:00 A.M. and he made a mental note that as soon as he had Dr. Hamilton secured in the conference room, he would dash to the front door and capture her before she wandered into the hostile camp.

As he headed down the corridor, the halls were buzzing. Something had happened to Judge Taylor and he was in the hospital. Sean bumped into Ed Sheridan who assured him that Judge Taylor had been hospitalized because of high blood pressure but the trial would proceed as scheduled. Sean breathed a sigh of relief. He knew his most critical witness, Dr. Hamilton, could only testify that day and would not be available at all after that. He had moved his entire operating schedule to Wednesday in order to accommodate his testimony. Dr. Grouper was now away on a trip and Dr. Hamilton was managing the clinic as well as shouldering total responsibility for not only his surgeries, but for Dr. Grouper as well.

Sean tried to be as casual as possible with Dr. Hamilton as they spoke in the conference room. He was, however, nonplussed by Dr. Hamilton's casual appearance. He did not dress the part of a prominent pediatric physician and world-renown surgeon, preferring khaki pants, a fading blue shirt and a non-descript tie loosely knotted at the collar. Sean noticed that the young doctor carried all his belongings and medical records in a beat up backpack slung over his shoulder. Sean was glad that he had requested to see him in the conference room. This way, no member of the jury could see the doctor's casual and informal appearance. Cases are won or lost on little things, and sometimes lost in the courtroom corridors before the witness even testifies. Sean was quite aware of what kind of initial impression his leading medical witness would make on the jury, particularly if they saw him carrying a green backpack over his shoulder like a young school-boy. His testimony, thus, would be given the weight of a student and not that of a prominent board certified professional.

After fifteen minutes chatting with Dr. Hamilton, Sean left him alone in the conference room reviewing hospital records and went to check for the arrival of Ms. Paula Murray, Lisa's teacher. He knew she would be right on time, right on schedule. Teachers were always on time. Sean looked down the corridor and saw a very attractive woman entering the front door. She was medium height, smartly dressed, in her late twenties, and had long black hair, rosy cheeks, a very healthy outdoor complexion, and blue eyes. Sean approached Paula Murray and greeted her warmly. She was very polite and said that she was happy to be in court and that she would do what she could to help Lisa. She told Sean she had that morning just delivered to the Clerk of Court all of Lisa's subpoenaed school and medical records. Sean felt immediately relieved that the records were now in good hands.

Chapter 15

Trial Errors

Sean knew that Judge Taylor would be in error if he prohibited Dr. Hamilton, a nephrologist, from testifying as an expert against a specialist in another field, in this case Dr. Smith and Dr. Blade, who were pediatricians not nephrologists. Challenging Judge Taylor would make him livid with rage; and a raging Judge Taylor would be a Judge Taylor out of control. It would serve Sean's purpose, though.

Trial lawyers instinctively push the envelope as far as they can. Sometimes they even try to put in more evidence than they should. Sean knew it was probably hopeless and certainly risky to take chances but, in order to be successful, you had to take risks. Now he desperately wanted to trap Judge Taylor, on the record, on an error of law so that if he lost the case, he might be able to appeal and have another chance to win. It would be like buying a little insurance. He knew that any time you challenge a trial judge, he knows you are trying to provoke him into making errors of law. This can have devastating consequences.

At this point in the case Sean wanted to demonstrate to the jury that Judge Taylor was hostile and prejudicial to the plaintiff. He was hoping the jury would recognize that this hostility prevented Judge Taylor from being fair. Challenging the judge was a calculated gamble but an appropriate strategy under the circumstances. But his confidence left him immediately when he saw the rage on Judge Taylor's face as both counsel approached the bench. The judge began screaming about how unqualified Dr. Hamilton was and he couldn't testify in the area of pediatrics and urology because he was not a board certified pediatrician nor a board certified urologist. The harangue continued and could be heard by everyone within ten miles of the courthouse. He ranted and raved in front of a very attentive, disturbed jury.

Sean told Judge Taylor that he would not press for the admission and would simply note his objection. But the raving continued. Sean knew that the judge would make him pay for any small successes of the previous day. Taylor seemed clearly intent on destroying any semblance of Sean's case, and it was obvious to the defense counsel that Sean had made a tactical blunder. Judge Taylor was exacting a heavy price.

The judge screamed for what seemed an eternity. However, Sean knew that Taylor could not prevent Dr. Hamilton from testifying as a causation witness as to the ravages of Lisa's kidney disease.

So he switched gears and told the judge that he
would not be introducing Dr. Hamilton as a liability
expert due to the Judge's exclusionary ruling but
simply as a medical causation witness. Taylor
could not legally disqualify Dr. Hamilton as a
medical causation witness since he was board
certified and a nationally recognized authority on
kidney diseases and treatment. Even Judge Taylor
had to consider Hamilton an expert in kidney
diseases and treatment and allow him to testify as to
the level of kidney injury suffered by Lisa.

With Taylor's angry tirade over for now,
Sean resumed his direct examination, his
confidence slowly returning. Dr. Hamilton, in clear
and precise words and referring to anatomical charts
and drawings, described to the jury the progression
of Lisa's kidney disease over the six-year period.

Sean spent a great deal of time describing
the injury and damage aspect of the case with his
expert. It was apparent to all that the jury was
listening intently and following Dr. Hamilton's
testimony closely. Dr. Hamilton's appearance
might have been disorganized but his medical
knowledge and professional bearing were winning
over the jury. Most jurors were leaning forward,
their eyes transfixed on Dr. Hamilton. Sean spent a
great deal of time describing kidneys, kidney
dialysis and how it works, why it's necessary, and

why the blood has to be circulated for the kidneys to function. He emphasized that dialysis is only a temporary measure and how being linked to a machine is fraught with deadly complications such as infection, stroke and death. He explained that the patients can have seriously adverse reactions to the medications, and that much pain and suffering is involved when the blood goes through the system. Finally, he had Dr. Hamilton discuss how a transplant takes place and whether or not Lisa had any hope for a successful transplant in the future. Sean knew he did well before the jury. Now the jurors were nodding their heads with sympathy for Lisa. It seemed that any damage inflicted by Judge Taylor had been diffused, at least for the moment.

Sean glanced at the clock. It was 11:00 A.M. He had promised to have Dr. Hamilton back at the hospital that afternoon at 2:00 P.M. He needed to wrap up his exam and allow the cross-examination so that Dr. Hamilton would be able to complete his testimony in full that day. Sean finished his direct by asking Dr. Hamilton to confirm that all injuries Lisa suffered were a direct result of her kidney condition. Due to Dr. Hamilton's limited time commitment, it was now time to end the direct abruptly. Sean had deliberately timed it so that the defense counsel would have an hour to cross-examine Dr. Hamilton as, under normal circumstances, this would be more than adequate for the defense. Sean, however, had underestimated Judge Taylor's cunning and unpredictable scheduling antics. As soon as Sean finished his direct, Judge Taylor turned to the jury and gasped that he was not feeling well and required an additional thirty-minute recess, although he was looking healthy as a horse. Under the circumstances, the thirty-minute recess was a kiss of death for completing Dr. Hamilton's testimony that day. It would now be impossible and he could not possibly return the next day. Sean glanced over and saw Attorney Howe smile at his coterie of young attorneys and paralegals, who had brightened up considerably, becoming very animated. They were smiling derisively at Sean. He knew Attorney Howe and the defense team were now on the verge of winning the battle of experts. It was a chess game and Dr. Hamilton was being eliminated from the board. Attorney Howe would certainly take more than an hour in his cross-examination of Dr. Hamilton and, if necessary, would waste any additional time on some collateral or unnecessary matter. It was now certain that Dr. Hamilton would have to come back the next morning and, if he did not or could not testify, Judge Taylor would be more than happy to dismiss all his previous testimony and gladly instruct the jury to disregard it. This would be a fatal blow to the plaintiff's case as Lisa did not have any chance of winning her medical case without Dr. Hamilton's testimony.

Chapter 16

The Vanishing Witness

Judge Taylor banged his gavel promptly at 1:00 P.M. Dr. Hamilton contritely blurted out to the judge, "Sorry, Your Honor, but I won't be able to return tomorrow because of my heavy operative schedule. This will not jeopardize the case, will it?" Judge Taylor angrily responded loud enough for all to hear, particularly the jury, "Doctor, if you can't return, that's quite all right. That won't present any problems. But, regrettably, I'll have to strike all your previous testimony and instruct the jury to disregard it." Taylor then loudly cracked his gavel startling everyone, particularly Dr. Hamilton who was quite taken aback and his face was now red with emotion and seemed to be very perplexed. Taylor: "Court is adjourned until tomorrow promptly at 9:00 A.M."

Sean managed to console the disturbed Dr. Hamilton as best he could. "Doctor, you have done your best. If you can't return, that is O.K. We know your young patients need you and their operations can't be delayed. They are life saving operations." "Sean, I'm so sorry," he said. "I tried my best to help Lisa. Is it true that if I don't testify tomorrow, all my testimony will be stricken? What if I come the day after tomorrow?" Sean, "No, unfortunately Judge Taylor will not allow it. Perhaps another judge would but not Taylor. If you don't testify tomorrow at 9:00 o'clock, all your testimony will be dismissed. This is how trials are conducted and why the judge, not the witnesses, controls the trial. If you don't return, the jury will be instructed to disregard all your testimony, not to consider it, and to cleanse it from their minds. It would basically be the same if you didn't appear in court at all." Dr. Hamilton said, "I can't leave Lisa in the lurch. Too much is at stake. I'll do something. I must do something. I'll try to get here tomorrow at 9:00. I'll do my best." Sean said, "Thanks for everything you've done. If you can't make it tomorrow at 9:00, don't worry about it. You've already done more than your share and Lisa and the Rowes are so grateful." Needless to say, Sean did not sleep well that night. All he could think of was whether or not Dr. Hamilton would be able to make it to court at 9:00. He would know tomorrow. It was out of his hands.

Sean arrived at the courthouse an hour before 9:00. He exchanged pleasantries, as always, with Ed Sheridan and tried to project his usual upbeat attitude. Attorney Howe and his managerie of attorneys and paralegals were smiling and having a lot of fun joking in the corridor. Sean could see that, when he glanced over at them, they were actually laughing derisively at him. It was ten minutes to 9:00. The case was now in the balance. Sean knew that Dr. Hamilton's testimony would be dismissed in the next ten minutes and Lisa would lose her case if Dr. Hamilton was not in court promptly at 9:00. The hour struck. Sean slowly went down the aisle and approached counsel's table. The Howe defense team was already seated and was in high spirits. Their laughter and small talk filled the courtroom. They were jubilant.

At 9:00 Judge Taylor dove into the courtroom. For the first time since the case started he was smiling and seemed happy with the anticipated outcome. He sensed that the end was near. He was also enjoying the prospect of Sean's upcoming disbarment and potential malpractice claim against him. Sean knew that the end was in sight. He had played his last card and had no other hope of squeezing out any time continuances. Behind Sean were seated Lisa and the Rowes with their heads down. They were expecting the worse as were all the spectators. The Clerk, Ed Sheridan, was no longer smiling. He was fiddling with papers with his head down and tears appeared to be in both eyes. A tragedy was now taking place in the courtroom. Taylor loudly gathered the court to order. "Bailiff, send for the jury. Trial counsel immediately approach the bench." Taylor to McArthur, "Are you aware that presently it does not appear that Dr. Hamilton is here? Since he is not here, once the jury is seated, I will be compelled to instruct the jury to disregard all his testimony and if his testimony is dismissed, I understand that you'll not be able to present any further medical testimony. The case will then have to be dismissed. Do you get my drift? Will you now voluntarily dismiss the case without having me do so for you?"

Sean was speechless, bent over, heartbroken. What could he do? The ceiling in the courthouse was like a vise, slowly closing in on him. He seemed to be losing his sense of reality. Was his case really about to be lost? Could this be happening? He thought people facing eminent death must feel like this. What can they do to change their fate? The case was about to collapse and Lisa would never get her day in court.

The parade of jurors slowly entered the courtroom and their faces were sober but alert as they meticulously searched the courtroom for Dr. Hamilton. He was not to be found. One could see they sensed the worse. Their service as jurors was about to come to an end. Taylor now smiled and addressed the jury, "Members of the jury, I now have the judicial obligation to advise you that you are to disregard ...." Before Judge Taylor could

utter another word, Dr. Hamilton swung the
courtroom door open and, with a rush that was
noticeable to all, raced into the courtroom as if he
were finishing the last leg of a marathon. His face
was red and sweaty, his tie was loose and his suit
jacket was askew. He raced up to Sean and in a
barely audible gasp muttered, "Can I take the
stand?"

Judge Taylor seized the moment, "Dr.
Hamilton, you are late! You know my court starts
at 9:00. All witnesses are supposed to be here at
9:00. Just because you're a doctor, that does not
give you special priority. In the future you are to
appear promptly. Do you understand me, doctor?"
Dr. Hamilton meekly responded, "Yes. I apologize
but I had operations this morning and one severe
complication and it ran rather late. I had to stay to
protect the patient. I'm very sorry I wasn't here at
9:00. I tried my best." The jury, hearing this
response, smiled. You could see that at that
moment Dr. Hamilton had won their hearts.

Sean, now elated, also tried to seize the
moment and, in a very authoritative voice, directed
Dr. Hamilton to "Please take the stand." Judge
Taylor, in a rage, blurted out, "Mr. McArthur, who
you do you think you are? It's not your function to
tell or direct witnesses to take the stand. That's my
function and mine alone and you know it.

Remember, I run this courtroom not you. Doctor, I'm the one that gives directions in this courtroom and you may take the stand but, in the future, just because you're a professional, that does not excuse you from being on time when you come to my court. Remember your tardiness and disrespect is noted. I must instruct you in the future not to be late for court and not to be disrespectful to the jury and to the Court. You may take the stand."

Attorney Howe slowly and solemnly rose to continue his cross-examination. His questions were simple and routine and were easily handled by Dr. Hamilton, who responded confidently to each. One could tell immediately that the jury was satisfied with his answers as Dr. Hamilton showed his depth and vast knowledge of his medical specialty, diagnosing and treating kidney disease. Each time Dr. Hamilton responded to one of Howe's questions, the jury leaned over to listen. They seemed to be impressed with Dr. Hamilton's detailed and distinct responses and his ability to make the complex appear simple. He had a knack for making the complex anatomy of a kidney very simple and understandable. Dr. Hamilton's integrity, medical knowledge and sincere approach were winning positive jury points and Howe knew it. But he amazingly, continued to ask the doctor medical questions.

Dr. Hamilton's selflessness and dedication to his patient, Lisa, and his overcoming impossible odds to come to court despite a tremendously busy operating schedule, also won him the jury's favor. Hamilton, in response to medical questions, was giving clear and precise testimony concerning the dangers of Lisa's life-threatening condition. Attorney Howe was losing on each question he asked. Sean was praying to himself for Howe to continue questioning. However, even Howe knew the questioning was a losing proposition and stopped.

At the end of Howe's questioning of Dr. Hamilton, it was clear that the defense had suffered a setback. The defense team looked stone faced and dumb struck. They were clearly unhappy with the results of the cross-exam. Dr. Hamilton had won the day and one could tell from the positive response from the jury that he was now not only winning the hearts but their minds as well. Lisa's case, rather than being totally finished , was alive and well, at least for one more day.

Chapter 17

Outfoxing the Fox

It was essential that experts be familiar with all medical components of the case before called to the stand. Sean knew they would be severely cross-examined, and if they had not reviewed all of the pertinent and relevant medical records, their credibility would be destroyed and Lisa would lose her case.

Judge Taylor's rigidness in requiring Sean to identify each and every one of his experts the day before trial put the defense and Chauncy Howe in a very favorable position: They had more time to prepare a major cross-examination strategy for each witness. In effect, they would be well prepared and ready to attack each witness.

The element of surprise was lost. Any witness Sean identified would be severely and skillfully examined by a well-prepared defense counsel, and any element of chance was greatly diminished. Defense counsel knew in advance the identity of Sean's witnesses, which greatly weakened his case. He usually relied on a certain element of surprise and drama, and he often did the unexpected. Now he knew he was arguing this unbelievably complex medical case from his boot straps. Neither he nor his experts had access to the defendants' medical records or to the Savin HMO records. Sean was trying this case not only without a compass but without even a medical rudder.

He sat despondently at counsel table and pondered what to do. Court would only be in session a half day, from 9:00 A.M. to 1:00 P.M. Sean was under strict judicial orders to have his witnesses lined up in order each day. He had to prepare continually each day for four hours of live testimony. Judge Taylor was a stickler and demanded that the case move quickly and expeditiously. Sean knew if there were any breaks in his testimony, if he was not prepared to have his witnesses ready, one after the other, Judge Taylor would very happily entertain a Motion to dismiss his case. After Lisa and Dr. Hamilton testified, Sean would take the calculated and dangerous risk of calling Dr. Smith as his next witness. Sean knew this was a gamble but he decided it would be impossible to prove his case without cross-examining Dr. Smith and Dr. Blade. Sean was now breaking all the rules and hoping for the best. He was walking on the edge, trying his case in the fast lane. There was no margin of error.

He realized that putting Dr. Smith and Dr. Blade on the stand was a calculated risk and could boomerang against him if he fell flat on his face and was unsuccessful in his cross-examination. Sean knew his cross-examination of the defendants could win or lose the case. The case was now at the most critical juncture.

Jurors rely on first impressions but, unfortunately, often have the attention span of the average MTV viewer. Jurors are generally impatient, time conscious, want quick answers and vivid presentations. If the jurors concluded, on first impression that Dr. Smith was credible after Sean's cross-examination and if he was not totally damaged by Scan's cross, a majority of them would find the doctor medically credible. They would have confidence in him and his testimony and would quickly conclude that what he did for Lisa was medically sound and he was not at fault nor acted below the standard of care. The jury's initial leaning toward the defense would be a disaster and could extinguish the light in Sean's case before it even was ignited.

Sean, as was his practice as an experienced trial attorney, mentally outlined his cross-examination of Dr. Smith based on the medicine he had been able to learn concerning kidneys and the tests and procedures that should have been done on Lisa in accordance with the standard of care. Because Dr. Smith' medical records had been withheld, Sean would have to improvise while he cross-examined Dr. Smith and had him review and analyze his records on the stand. This was no small feat especially with the short and ill-tempered trial judge prodding the attorney not to waste time reading records in front of the jury and not to be dilatory. Sean had to be very quick in his medical analysis and quickly find flaws within the medical records that were indicators of mistakes. There was no room for stumbling or mistakes on Sean's part. He would have to rely on his experience and trial instinct to quickly identify medical flaws as he saw them for the first time and was examining the witness in front of him before a demanding jury and an aggressive trial judge. Any missteps would not only infuriate and lose points with the jury but also Judge Taylor, who hated to see unprepared lawyers try cases in his presence. Sean was playing Russian Roulette with Dr. Smith's testimony. Sean knew that Dr. Smith was the most vital witness in the case. He would be a formidable opponent. Dr. Smith had been very well prepared and had been coached endlessly by his extremely talented defense team. Furthermore, Dr. Smith was an experienced medical witness as he had testified on numerous medical cases throughout the cases for doctors accused of medical malpractice and was a very savvy and experienced courtroom expert. He was a veteran of the courtroom and, in many ways, the courtroom was his stage. He knew how to handle any sophisticated questions and to answer so as to hurt the plaintiff's case and to advance the defendant's case.

Sean's chance of blowing Dr. Smith off the stand and quickly destroying his credibility on his cross was extremely remote, but Sean would do the best he could despite the odds. He had no other choice.

Judge Taylor burst onto the scene with his usual BANG and annoying clatter. Everyone in the courtroom was now accustomed to this piercing sound, but still it had a startling effect on anyone within earshot of Taylor's courtroom. Judge Taylor slammed his notebook down loudly, struck the gavel like a sledgehammer against the old dilapidated wooden desk that somehow survived the blow. In his usual angry voice, Taylor ordered the plaintiff's counsel to call his next witness. Sean glanced at the Rowes, gave them a friendly warm smile, nodded and then, in a calm, controlled, polite voice requested that Dr. Smith please take the stand.

Dr. Smith, tall and elegant, slowly rose from the first row of the spectator's bench directly behind defense counsel where most defendants sit in order to be close to their trial counsel and to the jurors. He had been seated between his wife, Melinda, a well-known benefactor in the community and

Richard Bishop, their minister. Dr. Smith had the look of a sophisticated patrician and, as he strode to the witness stand, Sean could tell that the doctor was used to being in control and in charge. Every pore of his body oozed confidence. As he walked, he looked around the courtroom, nodded confidently to his beautiful wife, his minister, his defense counsel. His steely blue eyes looked into those of each juror as he passed, and he seemed to be nodding to them as well. As he faced Judge Taylor, he gave a casual turn of his head and Judge Taylor reciprocated with a warm friendly smile. Sean found this strange. He had never seen Judge Taylor smile warmly at anyone. He reserved his smiles for the moment when defendants won another verdict in his courtroom.

Dr. Smith's crimson tie shone like a beacon against his well tailored blue striped Brooks Brothers suit. He dressed impeccably and was very impressive with his gray hair, graying mustache, and his rugged Marcus Welby good looks. He was certainly a very imposing figure who commanded attention.

Sean noticed that Judge Taylor's unkempt robe was drooping at half mast, and from the opening at the top, his identical crimson tie peeked out. It appeared that both ties were sending signals to one another. In a momentary flight of fancy,

Sean thought that Judge Taylor and Dr. Smith were probably sending secret coded messages through their ties. Taylor and Smith definitely looked like they were from the same club. It was apparent to all from their friendly glances that the two of them were friends, maybe from their Harvard days or from traveling in similar exclusive circles. Sean knew that both of them were long-time members and one-time officers of the Harvard Club, which was strictly for Harvard alumni, and noted for fine food, drink, and a place for high powered networking. It was known in Boston circles as a place to rub elbows, and to bend them.

Merely daring to call Dr. Smith early in the case as one of Sean's first witnesses had created excitement in the courtroom. This was an unusual tactic. Attorneys usually don't call hostile witnesses as their first witness. The jury now eagerly awaited Sean's examination. Dr. Smith was one of the key and pivotal witnesses, and had been accused of blatant malpractice in Sean's forceful opening statement, where he was identified as one of the medical villains who had ruined Lisa's life and caused her great suffering.

Sean initiated his examination in a methodical, controlled, but polite and conversational tone. He had Dr. Smith describe his medical care and treatment of Lisa and identify the records, tests, and studies he performed over the six-year period of treatment. Sean decided that politeness and friendliness were the number one ingredient for a successful examination. He did not want to be discourteous to Dr. Smith, or to antagonize the jury. Again, first impressions mean a lot.

As a skilled trial attorney, Sean knew that it would not be good tactics to attack Dr. Smith at this point. His approach would be one of smooth precision. Sean planned to kill this witness with kindness; a little honey is better than a lot of vinegar. Sean spent as little time as possible with the doctor's medical background and his education. He knew the defense would go over it in great detail and emphasize Dr. Smith's extensive and impressive credentials. Sean decided, "Why waste time adding to Dr. Smith's credibility?"

Sean also was aware that jurors disliked lawyers who are repetitive or who talk down to them, and he didn't want to upset them at the outset. So, Sean first had Dr. Smith acknowledge that he kept detailed and complete medical records on his pediatric patients. The doctor emphasized how he relied on the accuracy of his medical records. But, when Sean referred to the medical records and the lab tests, he noticed for the first time that Dr. Smith fidgeted and looked a little uneasy. Sean instinctively knew there was something in those records that was causing this unease and he sensed that Smith wanted to downplay the subject. Sean noted that he must keep this in the back of his mind. The records had suddenly become even more important. A number of times during the presentment of the records, the witness glanced nervously at his attorney. Sean requested to see the records and casually, one of Chauncy Howe's attractive female paralegals approached the witness stand.

No one in the courtroom, particularly the men on the jury, could help notice this striking young woman. She was a beautiful, blonde, athletic, well-tanned figure and was dressed in the modern style – in a tight fitting mini skirt. She smiled at Dr. Smith as she slowly handed him the medical records. Sean figured that Attorney Howe probably hired this bombshell in order to grab the jury's attention away from the seriousness of the case. This was a calculated tactic and the young woman played her role well. You could tell that the men on the jury had turned their collective attention away from the doctor and his medical records. They weren't thinking about kidneys any more.

The medical records were voluminous. You could tell by the size of the folders that Dr. Smith had seen Lisa over a long period of time. The records were marked, without objection, as the first exhibit in the case. Judge Taylor frowned at Sean. He knew that Sean had succeeded in putting in evidence that both the judge and Attorney Howe had been able to keep from the jury until that moment.

Sean, however, was all smiles. Now he would be able to introduce all of Dr. Smith's medical records and those records would, more than likely, win or lose Lisa's case. Without great fanfare, Sean had quietly and effectively taken the first critical step toward winning his case.

Sean now laid the foundation and, in summary fashion, quickly went over Lisa's six-year period of treatment with Dr. Smith. He particularly inquired regarding blood, urine, diagnostic, and dip stick studies that Dr. Smith had ordered for Lisa. Smith seemed proud of his treatment of Lisa and expressed confidence in the dip stick method to detect protein in Lisa's urine. Positive evidence of protein, of course, would be evidence of kidney disease and he proudly parroted he never found any positive evidence of kidney disease because all of the dip stick tests were negative. He stated firmly, with conviction, and on several occasions, that all his dip stick studies were negative. He seemed to put great emphasis upon this and he reemphasized it each time Sean referred to them.

Sean now had in his hands the actual dip stick studies, which he had never seen before. Sean did not understand how this was possible, as his kidney expert, Dr. Hamilton, was certain that because of Lisa's chronic kidney problems, she would have to have tested positive at some point over that period of time. Sean clearly could not attack or cross-examine Dr. Smith's credibility on this question because the medical records Sean held in his hand definitely supported Dr. Smith and his firm assertion that all Lisa's dip stick studies over the last six years were negative for protein in her urine.

Sean, rather than to emphasize winning defense points to the jury, quickly switched gears. He asked Dr. Smith about whether or not Mr. and Mrs. Rowe were conscientious about keeping their appointments over the six-year period. Dr. Smith had to concede that the Rowes seemed to be very good parents and were extremely conscientious about bringing Lisa to all of her scheduled visits. In fact, the record indicated that she did not miss one scheduled visit over that six-year period. Sean also had Dr. Smith concede that Lisa took all her medications and underwent every lab test he recommended, and that she always, over the six year period, went to Savin Medical Labs with her urine samples in order to be tested for protein. Dr.

Smith also conceded that Mr. and Mrs. Rowe were extremely confident in him and trusted him completely during Lisa's time in his care. They had never questioned him or had a cross word with him concerning his treatment plan.

Dr. Smith was beginning to look like the ideal pediatrician. The jury was obviously very impressed and was nodding in approval each time he spoke about his level of care and his thoroughness. The jury had that knowing look like they already understood that the good doctor had done everything he could for Lisa, and strictly in accordance with proper medical procedure. Dr. Smith described how over the six-year period he would always consult with his associate, Dr. Blade, if there was a problem and also how he was never reluctant to send Lisa for urine tests at Savin Medical. Sean sensed that the two highly educated engineers on the jury who had scientific backgrounds were being snowballed by Dr. Smith and his medically detailed testimony.

The jury, in unison, was now leaning over their chairs in rapt attention. Some jurors even nodded in agreement as Dr. Smith explained the thoroughness of his medical tests. Everyone in the courtroom sensed that Sean's examination was falling flat. Instead of questioning the doctor's credibility, each question seemed totally ineffective and was enhancing and supporting Dr. Smith's position. Dr. Smith was coming across as golden and was the best witness on his own behalf. One could quickly see that any sympathy or support the jury had for Lisa was dissipating. The jury liked Dr. Smith. The tide was turning irreversibly in the direction of the defense, and the structure of Sean's case was being demolished.

Sean sensed that the jury was not impressed with his shaky cross-examination but he persisted. Sean's strategy at that juncture in the trial was to have Dr. Smith admit that, while he did all the appropriate blood tests, consults, and referrals, despite these tests over a six-year period, he still could not diagnose that Lisa had a chronic kidney condition that had existed over the entire six years. Sean would try to make hay out of the fact that this kidney condition did not just happen overnight but was chronic and long term and went on over a long period of time. The jury thought Sean was losing the case but he was setting the stage for his next aggressive move.

To address the injury component of Lisa's case, Sean had Dr. Smith concede that Lisa had lost a great deal of time from school over the six-year period. However, Dr. Smith countered that any time lost by Lisa had little to do with her kidney problem but was simply due to sporadic colds and viruses. Dr. Smith seemed to have a snappy answer for each one of Sean's questions and always responded with beaming confidence. He was brimming with confidence. Sean's case was sinking fast. Dr. Smith was making a favorable impression as an expert. He was definitely pitching a shutout and Sean was scoring no points. His cross was useless.

Chapter 18

Challenging the Defense

Sean continued with his unexciting but persistent cross. This was his last chance and he knew it. Sean knew he had only one card to play. That card was concessions made by the doctor. He had very few points that he could attack except on the question of Dr. Smith's following urine tests on Lisa over a six-year period of time and not finding any positive results. He started asking Dr. Smith what significance was attached to a finding of protein in the urine. He spent many minutes on this subject and his repetitive questions were boring the jury, and even the witness. Dr. Smith, each time the question was posed, answered confidently, "If there was ever protein in the urine, the standard of care would require that the patient be referred immediately to a nephrologist for a kidney evaluation and the failure to do so would be a violation of the medical standard of care."

Dr. Smith had not found any test that indicated Lisa had protein in her urine. Sean was whipping a dead horse. His persistence in reviewing the numerous urine studies over a six-year period ad nauseum was severely weakening his cross-examination to the point where it was not only

dull, and inept but was terribly boring. Judge
Taylor was leaning forward on his desk glaring,
getting redder by the moment and ready to explode.
The jury was bored and was becoming restless.
Sean was praying like a fighter who had been
stunned by a vicious punch waiting for the bell to
ring. Sean was hoping and praying for the morning
break.

At approximately 11:30, Judge Taylor, with
his blood pressure rising and needing a medication
break, suddenly interrupted and told the jury it was
time for the morning break. Dr. Smith triumphantly
exited the stand to the smiles and admiration of the
jury and the confident defense team. Almost
everyone in the courtroom, spectators included,
found him to be an exceptionally professional
medical witness – honest, bright, direct, and caring.
Dr. Smith had presented himself as the perfect
pediatrician. To the jury and the courtroom
spectators, it seemed that Sean's cross-examination
was senseless, an embarrassment, a disaster.

As the courtroom noisily emptied, Sean
observed how the Rowes looked totally dejected.
Their heads were bowed, a sign of defeat and
resignation. Their body language said it all: Sean
had failed miserably in his cross-exam of Dr. Smith
and Lisa's case was hopeless; no jury could ever

find him at fault based on his flawless presentation and Sean's ineffective cross-examination.

The courtroom was empty and Sean sat lost in thought. His case had no hope. He needed a miracle. He silently prayed for inspiration. Ed Sheridan wandered over: "Sean, you're lucky. We put this stuff away for safe keeping last night. One of Howe's cronies came in and wanted to go through all of the medical records from Lisa's school. I told him he couldn't because they were locked up. This eager beaver came again this morning. I told him again, in very strong language, that they were not available because Judge Taylor would not allow records to be released.

This obnoxious whippersnapper finally gave up the hunt. Now I have the actual records you wanted, Amigo. I kept them in my possession so they wouldn't be 'misplaced'. You know how this can happen. I've seen it happen more than once myself. Well, not this time. Here are the goods, the real McCoy. Thank God for Lisa's teacher. Use it wisely. And, Sean," he paused, "Damn the torpedoes and watch out for Taylor!" Ed winked, smiled broadly, and sauntered out of the courtroom.

The courtroom was still empty, stone silent. Sean carefully inspected the records Ed had left. After a few minutes, Sean realized that Ed had given him all of the urinalysis tests Ms. Murray had brought from Lisa's school. Most of the pages were copies of the urine tests. Sean glanced at what he thought were copies but was amazed to find, in full view, four original urinalysis tests. These original studies, which Sean now held in his hands, were all positive for finding protein in Lisa's urine.

Sean felt faint. He felt his heart pounding. He was starting to hyperventilate. He thought he would drop on the spot. He looked around nervously and hoped no one was observing him in this panicked state. He was now holding the most incriminating evidence, the smoking gun, the key to winning Lisa's case. He had one last shot at examining Dr. Smith, the most critical witness. He still had him on the stand and was now ready to attack and, he hoped, to spring the trap. He did not have much time. He wondered if Dr. Smith would accommodate him and take the bait. Timing was everything now. Although he was alone, Sean felt like he was being watched by a thousand eyes. Was he getting gun shy? Did he have the courage and trial ability to succeed, to annihilate Dr. Smith's credibility with the evidence he held in his hand?

At 11:45, Judge Taylor came crashing back into the courtroom as usual, using noise and surprise to herald his staggering appearance and to shock everyone within earshot to attention. This time Sean was not rattled but glanced languidly at

the judge and asked, "May I proceed?" Judge
Taylor glared coldly at Sean and nodded reluctantly.
Sean knew he would not be given more than a few
minutes to complete his cross-examination. Like
any good poker player, Sean didn't want to give
away his hand or reveal prematurely what his next
move would be. Any aggressive or unusual move
would surely tip off the defense. Judge Taylor,
always trying to be flip, inquired impatiently,
"Haven't you had enough time to examine this
witness? How much longer will you take? Your
exam is repetitious. I'll give you no more than five
minutes and that's it. You have had too much time
already." Taylor was again embarrassing Sean in
front of the jury and his sharp questions were
definitely accomplishing their purpose. Taylor's
allegiance to the defense and his hostility to Sean
was becoming obvious and his partisanship was
definitely showing. But the jury seemed to be in
sympathy with Judge Taylor because they looked
like they too thought Sean didn't have a case. Sean
was merely persecuting an innocent defendant.
Taylor was again using his whole arsenal of
weapons and was doing anything he could to disrupt
Sean's timing and tempo. Sean knew he had to act
quickly.

Sean casually approached Dr. Smith and
asked him to review his urinalysis studies one more

time. Sean glanced toward the bench and saw Taylor's face getting redder. The clock was ticking. But this time Sean had in his hand the four original positive urine studies. Sean shuffled the pages of urine studies and innocently handed the doctor several of them. Dr. Smith, ever smiling, described the first four copies as negative.

Sean calmly dipped into the new pile of the original urinalysis studies that Paula Murray had been subpoenaed to bring to court the day before. This time, standing directly in front of Dr. Smith, Sean meticulously picked out the four **original** studies. He tried to be physically and emotionally calm but he felt exhilarated, like he was playing high stakes poker with card sharks and he was slowly and methodically shuffling the deck so the right cards would be on top when he dealt the critical hand. "Doctor, I would like you to look further at some of these urine studies that took place over the six-year period that you treated Lisa. Please look in particular at the urine studies done in January, 1996, February, 1995, May, 1994, and December, 1993."

Dr. Smith accepted the papers and, as he perused each page, his patrician attitude underwent an amazing physical transformation. Suddenly he paled, his body seemed to sag, and the panic in his eyes belied any residual arrogance. He was afraid and visibly shaken. In fact, he looked like he was about to have a stroke. The jury's demeanor went from a collective stupor to high alert at this unexpected development. Their eyes were transfixed on the crumbling patrician before them and they wondered what had suddenly altered Smith's demeanor.

Dr. Smith shot a frantic and desperate look at defense counsel but was not reassured by what he saw. He and his bewildered attorney exchanged a confused frightened look. Howe sensed immediately that something had gone terribly wrong but had no idea what it was. He was under the impression that Sean was simply repetitiously reviewing the negative urine studies. As far as Howe and his defense team knew, there was nothing to worry about because these studies would reveal nothing new. All of the studies Howe had delivered to the clerk's office were negative. Sean had somehow ambushed the defense and caught them napping. Sean quickly and decisively directed Dr. Smith's attention to the four **original** urine studies and asked him to read aloud to the jury the dates and their findings. Sean made certain his voice was loud pitched and authoritative to awaken any inattentive jury member. Sean: "Are the findings of these tests positive or negative?" In a barely audible whisper Dr. Smith replied, "They are all positive."

For a moment the courtroom went stone silent and then the jury gasped and rumblings could be heard in the spectator section. Dr. Smith's life was crumbling in open court. He was now being humiliated before one and all. The jurors, obviously shocked at this new development, stared slack jawed in total disbelief. Their icon, their hero had fallen. Attorney Howe looked dumb struck and traumatized.

Dr. Smith's devastating admission had exploded with the most incriminating pivotal evidence in the case. Now, everyone in the courtroom knew with certainty that in all probability the defendants, Dr. Smith, Dr. Blade and Savin Medical, had clearly and most certainly misdiagnosed Lisa's case over a six-year period. Her medical providers had not taken the care to follow up the four positive urine tests that were clearly documented over several years, and were likely responsible for Lisa's current life-threatening condition. Their bad medicine had put Lisa's life in jeopardy.

As a good trial lawyer, of course, Sean did not want to stop or let the witness off the hook at this point. He wanted to completely destroy Dr. Smith's credibility as an expert witness. He was aiming for the jugular but he had to be careful and precise. He didn't want to give the defense any time to recover and the opportunity to present any misleading explanations as to the discrepancy in the urine tests. Now was the time to strike and Sean knew it. Without missing a beat he quizzed Dr. Smith, who was still in a daze. He queried, "Dr. Smith, if there had been any positive findings in the urine studies over the six-year period, would it have been a violation of the standard of pediatric care not to have referred Lisa to a nephrologist?" The doctor's head was hanging, his breathing labored. He looked up at Sean, defeat and humiliation in his eyes. "Yes," he whispered in a barely audible voice. "Yes, it would have been." The fatal blow had been struck.

Sean dramatically stopped his exam and stared in disbelief at Dr. Smith. Then, ever so slowly, he walked past the entire defense team, after pausing for a moment directly in front of them to give them a slight contemptuous smile, and seated himself casually at counsel table. The deed had been done. Dr. Smith's credibility had been destroyed. Sean glanced defiantly at Judge Taylor. Taylor was seething with anger and shaking his head. He, too was amazed at the sudden turn of events. He, probably wondered how Sean had managed to outmaneuver the entire defense team and wondered how any experienced defense team would be so stupid and inept to have overlooked four positive urine studies. Sean knew why they had missed them and he made eye contact with Ed Sheridan and smiled. Ed met his eyes with a satisfied Cheshire cat smile. Sean had delivered a clear and decisive blow and it was now obvious to all, particularly the jurors, that the missing records were the fatal flaw in the defense case. Dr. Smith and Dr. Blade's defense was based on a lie and it had now been totally demolished.

Attorney Howe, after Sean's cross, slowly rose to re-direct and to attempt to rehabilitate his fallen witness. What could he do to salvage his witness after this withering and deadly cross-examination? All the cool cockiness had drained from Attorney Howe's body. He stood like a dazed boxer on the ropes awaiting the knock out blow. Howe was obviously unprepared to resurrect his prize witness and had no reasonable explanation for the positive urinalysis tests and the lack of follow-up on the part of both Drs. Smith and Blade. How do you defend a lie? Howe asked a few vague questions and then ended his re-direct. What else could he do without further incriminating his clients?

Howe had basically thrown in the towel. The jury would have more than ample credible evidence to find his clients negligent and responsible for all the kidney damage inflicted upon Lisa. As Dr. Smith limply exited the witness stand, Sean noted that some of the jurors gave him angry looks. Their previous warm smiles had faded. Several of the jurors were experienced engineers, very well versed in science and aware of the significance of scientific tests. These jurors seemed to be particularly disturbed with this new development. They had thought that Dr. Smith, practicing medicine as a science, could do no wrong and that he would follow the appropriate protocol for treatment. Now they looked puzzled and annoyed. Dr. Smith and the defense team had suddenly become villains in this morality play. Several of the women jurors had tears in their eyes and were visibly shaken. The jury definitely showed a positive shift in favor of the plaintiff's contention that Lisa had been improperly treated by her caretakers. After all, medical records don't lie, do they? The fatal flaw in the defense was now exposed and the more they tried to defend it, the more obvious the flaw became.

The court clock showed ten minutes to adjournment. It seemed like an eternity. Attorney Howe looked furtively at the bench and asked to approach. In a quiet, shaky voice, he asked Judge Taylor if the court could adjourn for the day. Sean, from bitter past experience with Judge Taylor, knew if he had asked for a ten-minute delay, it would not be allowed and he would be lectured derisively. However, the friendly relationship between Judge Taylor and Chauncy Howe went back a long way. Judge Taylor, perhaps secretly hoping somehow that Howe could recover, muttered, "This is a reasonable request and I will allow it." Taylor glared at Sean who merely avoided any eye contact and looked away.

Sean was trying to figure out why Taylor was upset with him when he had just proved that the defense was lying. He always was mystified by Judge Taylor's reactions and total pro-defense bias. You could see the jury was now wising up and that they were very annoyed with Taylor's partisan tactics. The jury had lost respect for the defendants, the defense team, and for Judge Taylor. The jury had seen the light of day. They were angry at the partisan defense rulings and Sean could sense that he had won their sympathy.

"Ladies and gentlemen of the jury, it's been a long day. We'll come back tomorrow at 9:00 A.M. sharp!" Taylor weakly banged his gavel and stumbled out of the court room. He looked like a broken man himself. But was the case won?

Sean knew that the defense still had time to play a few more tricks and he wondered what strategy was up Chauncy Howe's sleeve as he left the courtroom. Sean had delivered a potentially fatal blow but Howe, a seasoned and crafty litigator, was not one to go down without a fight. You could hear the gentle rustle of the courtroom clearing as Sean returned to counsel table and methodically collected his papers, which were strewn all over the place. Sean liked to look busy. He invariably kept several medical texts and treatises on counsel table in full view of the jury thinking it would impress the jury on his preparation. He did not have co-counsel with him and always looked very much the loner, the underdog. He enjoyed this role. His table usually looked like a disaster area after examining several witnesses in court.

Sean couldn't restrain himself from giving Ed another wink and a warm smile as he literally floated from the courtroom. Ed had somehow saved his case by preventing anyone from tampering with, altering, or destroying the critical four original urine studies. Sean knew from experience that critical medical records had a way of disappearing. Missing and vanishing original records and other critical medical documents can be the kiss of death in a close medical case and Sean knew he had narrowly escaped this happening in Lisa's case. "Thank God," Sean murmured to himself.

Ed, evidently, had protected the four positive studies. He prevented them from getting into the wrong hands. Sean wondered what would have happened if these studies had fallen into the hands of the defense. Would they have been preserved by the defense team or would they have mysteriously disappeared? Would they still be available to the plaintiff the next day? This was interesting food for thought and Sean didn't want to think of what would have happened if the records were missing. Sean, after years of close calls and previous missing records, had developed a paranoia and simply did not trust anyone with important records, especially if these records could alter the outcome of the trial. Sean always said it isn't paranoia if it's true.

Everything seemed on track and Sean felt certain that he was on the way to winning the case. He just needed to control what was happening over the next few days. There was still room for error. Things changed fast in a court and one had to be ever vigilant. As he left the courtroom, he spoke briefly and warmly with the Rowes. They seemed to be relieved. He gave Lisa, his special friend, a kiss on the cheek and a warm hug, told her to keep praying, and that he was doing his best. He told the Rowes, "Even though good things happened today, we have to always think about tomorrow." Sean knew that cases change quickly and are not often won in one day. He may have won a battle but the battle is not over until the victory is won. He was looking forward to the next day with measured trepidation and concern wondering what trick the wily Chauncy Howe would come up with to poke holes in Sean's case. He knew he would be in for a few surprises.

Chapter 19

A Critical Cross

At home that evening, he diligently worked on his cross-examination for the next witness whom he anticipated would be Dr. Blade. He was also preparing his cross-examination of potential dream team of defendants' experts who would testify later. Sean knew he had to be prepared for surprises and he tried to keep a step or two ahead of the defense. Sean tried to be vigilant and resilient always. He thought that this was the essence of trial advocacy, to be able to respond to surprises and be prepared to improvise.

Late that evening, Sean's home phone rang, rousing him from physical and emotional exhaustion. He was surprised to hear Quigley's voice because he usually never called Sean at home. As usual, Quigley was calling from his mobile law office, a bar in London. Sean could hear the Chieftains playing in the background along with loud laughter and other barroom sounds. "Sean," he screamed into the phone, "How are things going on the case? Sorry Jamie disappointed you." Sean answered, "Things aren't going as well as can be expected without O'Reilly. We're on the verge of losing the case." Sean didn't feel he owed Quigley any explanation and he didn't in any way want to limit his suffering. In fact, he wanted to add to it. He knew his associate just wanted to know if the case was won, when he would receive his fee, and, if the case was lost, when he would be brought before the Board. That was the way Quigley's mind functioned. Quigley seemed satisfied with Sean's curt and disingenuous answer. He said he had been talking to Rosie and passed on a message that Chauncy Howe's office had called and had spoken to Rosie about the case. Howe would be talking to Sean tomorrow at court. Rosie also would probably drop by the court to give Sean moral support and counsel. Quigley concluded, as always, with an exhortation, "Give 'em hell, Sean!" Sean answered, "I'll hang in there."

After the call Sean felt apprehensive. He didn't want Rosie around when his case was being tried. Rosie was not involved in the case in any way and, when he was in the courtroom, he was egocentric, too casual, and liked to steal the show. Sean could see him prancing around the courtroom with an entourage of lawyers and pretty faces while he boasted about how he was helping to win Lisa's case. This was not the time for a circus in the courtroom. The case was still in doubt and was actually in a very vulnerable stage. The tide could turn either way. Sean gave himself a pep talk and told himself to concentrate only on his cross-examination and expert witnesses and to forget about Rosie. However, he had a restless sleep that night. He was more anxious about what would happen the next day when he should have been thinking about the witnesses at trial. He felt edgy that somehow Rosie would disrupt the case and cause problems. Sean's instincts were usually right.

He arrived in court at his usual early time of 7:00 A.M., having spent the drive in mentally preparing his cross-examination of Dr. Blade, the next most critical witness. Sean knew the cat was out of the bag and the element of surprise would not be as effective as against Blade. Blade would be ready and would have been coached in how to answer in reference to the positive positive urine studies. Sean had to tread carefully and be well prepared.

He decided he would use a variation of the tactic he employed with great results against Dr. Smith. He knew that his key points, although important, would not be as dramatic as they were in cross-examining Dr. Smith. Sean kept focused on a way to make his cross-examination interesting and appealing to the jury and to keep the witness nervous and off guard.

Fifteen minutes prior to the opening of court, Sean noticed Chauncy Howe in the corridor waving and signaling for him to come over. It was an arrogant gesture the way Howe beckoned to other people, sort of like commanding a dog to heal. Sean ignored Howe's condescending hand waving. He defiantly looked away to avoid being beckoned. He was not a dog. You could tell that Howe was not pleased by being shunned. Why make life easy for him? Finally realizing Sean was not going to heal, Howe casually walked over and blurted out, "Sean, I've spoken with Dr. Smith, Dr. Blade and Savin Medical, and also with your law partner, Rosie, about an offer. We're willing to offer $500,000 to settle this case as long as it's sealed and confidential. Rosie advised, as your partner, that he was very pleased with the offer. It's a very generous offer and it's in your clients' interest to resolve this case. Can we settle?"

Sean cringed at the paltry offer and the reference to Rosie, his partner. He was Rosie's associate, not his partner. He felt angry that Rosie would have the nerve to intrude himself into the trial and discuss settlement offers considering he knew nothing about the case and had not even been at the trial. Sean looked at Chauncy Howe and responded with cool hostility, "I'm not interested in your offer. The cost of hospital and medical treatments over Lisa's lifetime would be over millions of dollars. Unless you come into that range, which is realistic and fair, we're not interested. However, since you made the offer, and to make it official, I shall advise my clients. But, I can assure you that the Rowes are not likely to settle for that paltry amount. If I'm mistaken, I'll let you know. Otherwise, we're ready to continue the trial." As soon as Sean finished speaking, he saw Rosie racing towards him, his face dripping with perspiration and his red handkerchief flapping urgently. He looked like a commuter trying to catch the last train. From the look of his puffy face and blotchy eyes, Sean could tell that he was the worse for wear. He seemed uncharacteristically disheveled. Breathless from running, and way out of shape, Rosie gasped, "Did you speak to Chauncy Howe? Well, you settled the case didn't you?" Sean responded, "No, the case is not settled, the offer is not anywhere close to the value of the case. The offer is low and it's unrealistic. It wouldn't even cover Lisa's basic projected medical expenses. Why should I advise the Rowes to settle this case when we are on the verge of winning it? That would be stupid. The Rowes want to go to verdict and so do I." Rosie looking like a madman spat out, "It's not your case! You have to settle the case. You just have to. I'll tell Quigley. He wants this case settled. What do you think you're doing? You know you can't trust the jury. You never know what they'll do. Quigley's the trial attorney in charge of the case, not you. Stop acting like an idiot. You **must** settle the case!"

At that moment, Ed Sheridan loudly intoned, "Everyone back into the courtroom. Trial is to commence." Sean shot into the courtroom and quickly spoke to the Rowes explaining that Howe's offer was unrealistic and unfair in view of Lisa's high medical expenses. The Rowes readily agreed, as they had become fond of Sean and had implicit trust in his integrity. They knew he was dedicated to Lisa's case and would do what was best for her case. Mrs. Rowe replied, "Sean, we trust you. You do what you think is best for Lisa." When Chauncy Howe entered the courtroom, Sean quickly conveyed to him that the Rowes were not interested in the offer. Sean could see that Howe was very angry about losing this opportunity to buy his way out of a difficult case. Now he knew his clients could not get away with a cheap settlement.

However, as Howe entered the courtroom, Sean was surprised to see what a difference a day makes. Howe had regained his supreme confidence and looked like a different man from the day before. He was his cool and arrogant self. Sean authoritatively called Dr. Blade to the witness stand. He started his cross-examination methodically and went over the same questions he had asked Dr.

Smith. Sean had Blade describe how he cared for the patient, read all the studies and found them all to be negative. However, Dr. Blade firmly stated that **he** didn't find any protein in any of the urine tests and that all the tests he did had come back negative. It immediately occurred to Sean that Dr. Blade was, in effect, protecting himself and was, in effect, testifying against Dr. Smith, shifting the spector of negligence directly to his colleague. Even though the four original urine tests done by Savin Medical had been positive for protein, according to the previous day's testimony, Dr. Blade was now posturing that it was his partner, Dr. Smith, who did not follow the four positive studies over the six-year period with appropriate referral. By his stream of denials, Dr. Blade was trying to salvage his medical career, save his clinic, and, at the expense of his friend, shift all responsibility and blame directly and exclusively to Dr. Smith.

Sean immediately recognized that this blame shifting response would cause some confusion in the jury's mind. The jury was pondering, "Who did it? Which doctor was at fault? Was it Dr. Smith or Dr. Blade, who should have followed up the positive urine studies?" Sean was equally perplexed. The jury would have to choose between several responsible parties and determine which doctor was most responsible and culpable for Lisa's inadequate treatment.

Sean knew a divided jury could result in a disappointing, confused and unfair verdict. The jurors did not know, nor would they ever, that Dr. Smith, Dr. Blade and Savin Medical each had separate individual insurance policies for $15 million. A verdict against only one defendant would limit Lisa's ability to recover only against that particular defendant for the limits of that particular policy. In other words, if Sean won against Dr. Smith, he would only prevail for $15 million. But, if he prevailed against all three individually insured defendants, he could recover three times that amount or theoretically $45 million dollars. If Lisa were to win her medical expenses, hospital expenses, and dialysis expenses for the future, it was important for Lisa to win against all three defendants. A lot was at stake. Sean recognized that Howe's defense strategy was to sacrifice one client, Dr. Smith, and his $15 million dollar insurance policy, to save Dr. Blade and Savin Medical's $30 million dollar insurance policy. Millions of dollars of insurance coverage was now at stake and Attorney Howe was fighting desperately to make sure at least two of the defendants were not found negligent thus saving the defendants' insurers $30 million dollars.

Desperately needing to win against both Dr. Blade and Savin Medical, Sean asked Dr. Blade, "If positive protein was discovered in the urinalysis studies, would the next step be to follow up with a nephrologist?" Dr. Blade promptly agreed, "Yes. It would be necessary and would require an immediate follow-up." Now to nail Dr. Blade and Savin Medical: "Would you agree that if you had read any of these four positive urine studies, you would have referred Lisa to a nephrologist immediately, is that correct?" Dr. Blade again responded, "Yes. That is required practice." Sean walked to his seat looking coldly at Dr. Blade and equally coldly at the defense team.

Attorney Howe immediately rose and, in a strong, controlled voice asked, "Dr. Blade, did you ever know over the years that there were four positive protein studies? Dr. Blade answered, "No, I did not and if I did, I would certainly have followed up." Howe, "No further questions." Then, looking at the floor, Dr. Blade slowly retreated from the witness stand. Again, if body language and demeanor were any indicator, Dr. Blade acted like a loser, and possibly like someone who had not spoken the truth. As Dr. Blade exited, jurors were shaking their heads, not very pleased with the doctor's unconvincing testimony. They shot him hostile looks as he departed. If the jury's body language and their reaction was any indication of their response to his testimony, this certainly was not a positive sign for the defense.

Sean was sure that the jury was wondering, as he was, why Dr. Blade did not know anything about the four positive urine studies over the six-year period. After all, as Sean had repeatedly stressed in his cross-examination of Dr. Blade, hadn't all the urine studies over the six-year period been done at Savin Medical? Hadn't all these tests, including the positive tests, been done at Savin Medical under the direct personal supervision of Dr. Blade? Why wouldn't Dr. Blade, who ran the lab at Savin Medical for a number of years and profited from all the extensive lab studies, not know the results of his own studies on his own patient? Wasn't it his medical obligation as a treating physician to know those results? Sean sensed that Dr. Blade's evasive self-serving explanation, rather than shifting responsibility and blame solely to Dr. Smith, merely angered the jury further and made them more hostile to all the defendants.

In Sean's mind, Dr. Blade's futile attempt to shift blame to save himself and his wealthy HMO clinic, had merely thrown more gasoline on the raging fire, angered and upset the jury, and enhanced the potential for a huge plaintiffs' verdict.

Chapter 20

For All The Marbles

The fateful day had arrived, the day all trial lawyers dread. It was the final day of trial and the last opportunity to present the case to the jury. Sean knew he had to be at his best and that any error or last minute slip-up in his closing argument could cost him the case. It was also his opponent's last opportunity. Chauncy Howe would use every arrow in his quiver, and would call on his many successful jury trials to pull the case out from the fire. Howe had a slight edge in that he was supremely confident, and he knew his clients represented the cream of the social strata. The jury would be unlikely to rule against two highly respected doctors. Howe could give them any number of logical or convincing reasons to find for his clients.

Sean entered the courtroom and walked slowly to counsel table. He noted the buzz of anticipation and the general chatter in the overcrowded courtroom. It was standing room only. At times it took on a circus atmosphere. It reminded him of a passage he once read in a French novel describing an unruly crowd before the beheading of King Louis XVI. Sean tried to pull his thoughts back to the room and to think only of the case. He was faced with a limited opportunity to convince twelve lay individuals that Lisa was deserving of full compensation for her suffering.

Sean glanced around and made eye contact with Rosie, who was surrounded by the usual bevy of pretty women, seemingly representing every modeling agency in greater Boston. Rosie's vacant, dull answering look and his stiff body language telegraphed to Sean that he was very angry with him for not following his advice and settling the case. If looks could kill, Sean would have died on the spot. He looked away and moved on to the front of the courtroom, to the spectator's section, directly behind counsel table. This section was packed with Dr. Smith's and Dr. Blade's supporters. Sean noticed that they were no longer together as they had been throughout the trial, but now were now in separate rows and, a few rows apart at that. "The troops are definitely divided," Sean thought with an inner chuckle. At this point in the case, Dr. Blade was openly blaming Dr. Smith for not following up on the positive urine studies. Both doctors and their entourages were clearly unfriendly toward one another.

Sean noted that Dr. Smith's entourage had expanded. It now not only included his attractive and well-dressed wife, but also his five college-age children; three handsome blond young men wearing blue blazers and Harvard crimson ties, and two blond-haired, attractive, smartly attired young women. In addition, Dr. Smith's pastor and several other ministers had joined his group. Dr. Blade had his own entourage, including his wife and children, and also a black, smartly attired minister. Sean wondered if the presence of the minister was calculated to have an impact on the several black jurors.

The rest of the spectators behind the defendants were white-jacketed, eager young men and women who were clearly medical students or residents associated with Boston-area institutions. Included in the group were several well established Massachusetts physicians, even one of the "celebrity" physicians who frequently appeared on Boston TV as an expert on medical cases. He had a reputation for disliking plaintiff trial attorneys. Sean figured that if the numbers game meant anything, the crowd was definitely for the defense. He and Lisa were not the people's choice.

Before settling back at counsel table, he glanced to his right. He recognized the Rowes sitting in the far corner of the courtroom. He waved to them, then got up and walked back to Lisa and her parents. He smiled at them and gave Lisa a kiss on the forehead and tried to muster up a few words of encouragement: "Lisa, this is your day. I'll do everything I can. Keep praying. We all love you very much and we know God will be with you today."

Sean walked back to his table at the front of the courtroom. As he passed through the ranks of Howe's entourage for what he hoped was the last time, they seemed even more angry and arrogant than before. He defiantly marched by them, avoiding their cold stares, and simply nodded to Attorney Howe, who returned the nod as he took his seat at counsel table.

Sean knew the next hour would decide the case.

He had fifteen minutes to convince the jury. He tried to concentrate on his argument when, suddenly, Judge Taylor burst into the courtroom. At this point in the case Sean had thought this daily outburst wouldn't disturb him. But he was wrong; it always did, and today it seemed worse. Sean felt apprehension and nervousness in every fiber of his body. He felt like his mind would explode and his body evaporate. Throughout the trial, Judge Taylor had ruled against Sean every chance he had, and soon he would instruct the jury. Sean had no doubt that the instructions would totally favor the defense. The jury would hear something like, "Dr. Smith and Dr. Blade have great medical judgment and in case of doubt, remember that they were using their best,

not necessarily their **perfect,** medical judgment."
Sean knew that this "wide range of medical
judgment" charge could be the kiss of death in a
malpractice case. If the jury bought into this, they
would never find in favor of Lisa.

To throw another roadblock, Judge Taylor
had informed Sean that his closing, even though this
was a highly complex case, could be no more than
fifteen minutes. Sean figured that Howe would be
favored, as he was in his opening, with a
"generous" fifteen minutes that could translate
closer to twenty-five, but Sean would be firmly held
to fifteen. It was not fair and it gave the defense a
tactical advantage, but this is the way Judge Taylor
had played the game all the way through. Howe
had Taylor in the palm of his hands. And, what if
Attorney Howe played the "interruption game,"
which was often employed by seasoned defense
attorneys to eat into Sean's allotted fifteen minutes?
Howe knew how to play this game, and he played it
well.

Judge Taylor loudly gaveled the court to
order. Prior to argument he emphasized to the
jurors that, "whatever the plaintiff's attorney tells
you, his argument is not evidence. You can only
rely on the evidence introduced at trial." Although
this applied to both attorneys, Judge Taylor kept
stressing "plaintiff's attorney." The tenor of his

charge was unbalanced, distorted and unfair. He seemed to single out the plaintiff's attorney and give the jury the impression that whatever argument the plaintiff made was not to be trusted. This partisan instruction would certainly have a negative effect on Sean's presentation. The odds for Lisa winning this case under these hostile conditions were great and overwhelming.

Sean thought that perhaps Rosie was right. He should have settled the case. He could never win a case before an unfriendly, pugnacious, disturbed and arrogant judge. He hoped his belief in the ultimate reasonableness of the jury wasn't misplaced. Could he, in fact, win a jury trial before a hostile judge? He hoped that the daily barrage of hostile newspaper and TV pieces praising physicians in Massachusetts that had appeared throughout the trial had not severely prejudiced the jury in favor of the defendants. Had the recent Sunday feature praising Savin Medical as one of the best HMOs in the state, if not the country, played a role in biasing the jury in favor of Savin Medical?

Sean had wondered why Judge Taylor didn't instruct the jury to ignore the partisan leanings of the media, which had constantly reported favorably about physicians throughout the trial. Adverse media was just another way to torpedo and prejudice Lisa's case, and Judge Taylor had to know that the articles would have a negative effect on the jury. Yet, when Sean had brought this to his attention, Judge Taylor simply had said it was "not necessary to mention it to the jury as this would more than likely just highlight the articles that the jury may have not read." Sean thought to himself, "What stupid logic! Why not deal with something that would bias the whole trial and meet it head on? It didn't make sense that the jurors would not notice the hostile articles." But he knew that the more he questioned the judge, the worse it would be for him, and for Lisa.

Howe rose slowly. He paused. The tension in the courtroom was electrifying, even before he uttered one word. He moved slowly until he stood calmly in front of the jurors and, in a controlled voice, told them, "my clients are two of the best doctors in Massachusetts. They are very caring of their patients; they loved Lisa very much and did everything they medically could over many years to care for her. They never hesitated to see her, even made house calls on the weekends. They sent her for urine studies and always tried to do their best and always evaluated her thoroughly with the best medical resources available to them.

Dr. Smith and Dr. Blade never intended in any way to hurt Lisa and were shocked to learn that she had a chronic kidney condition." Howe kept repeating that the doctors "did everything they could within the scope of medical judgment to treat her, and they did their best and used their best judgment." Howe must have used the words "best judgment" at least twelve times. "Just because she was found to have a kidney condition later doesn't mean it had anything to do with a perceived lack of care by these dedicated doctors. They did not cause Lisa's condition."

By Sean's count, Howe's closing was now well over the allotted fifteen minutes. In fact, it had lasted for almost twenty-seven minutes. Sean glanced at his watch and then looked sternly at Judge Taylor, but to no avail. Come hell or high water, Taylor would not interrupt Howe's closing. Howe concluded by stating that "these two doctors, Dr. Smith and Dr. Blade, were in the front of the medical battle line. They did their best every day. They are the best we have in our state. Their reputation is unimpeachable and no one should fault these wonderful, dedicated physicians who give up their lives and enjoyment constantly to practice medicine and to give the best they can to their patients, while managing extremely difficult and unusual cases." Howe concluded, "These good doctors, good men, have spent valuable time away from their patients who need them in order to be in the courtroom to clear their names and reputations.

Dr. Smith, Dr. Blade and Savin Medical are eagerly looking forward to your favorable verdict. They need it to give them the strength and encouragement to carry on and to continue to help other needy patients throughout Massachusetts."

Howe sat down. You could not hear a pin drop in the courtroom. Judge Taylor looked exuberant. Sean had never seen him smile so brightly for such a long period of time. Taylor's blue eyes were glaring like beacons under his deep red complexion. The defense table returned his smile and they nodded confidently to one another. They were flush with success. Dr. Smith and Dr. Blade looked relaxed and relieved, and very content. Their families now seemed happy and relieved and began chatting with one another. Howe's argument had been effective and it had an obvious impact on the jury. Throughout the argument, Sean had glanced over to gauge their reactions. The jury seemed to respond to each word, uttered so smoothly, so effectively, so persuasively, from Howe's lips. If the case ended with Howe's final argument, it was obvious that Lisa would not prevail and the defendants would win.

Sean now faced a terrifying challenge. In fifteen short minutes, he would have to rebut the defense, not to mention overcome an anticipated hostile charge from a very pro-defense judge. The odds of winning were daunting. He fought back the urge to cave in to self-doubt and instead rose slowly to his feet. It was his turn to speak. He looked at Lisa for encouragement and glanced at Ed one last time for reassurance. He heard Ed whisper, "Give 'em hell, Sean." The words strengthened him.

Sean studied the jurors, standing for what seemed a minute but was probably only seconds. But, in these seconds he looked each juror in the eye. Before he said one word, Sean wanted to make direct contact and look into the heart and soul of each juror. Each was now so important, so significant, and each would be involved in the final decision. Sean looked at each one warmly and tried to convey confidence. The courtroom was silent and Judge Taylor again wore his familiar frown. Here was truly the proverbial calm before the storm.

Sean, sensing that the defense would try to interrupt him, quietly and intensely addressed the jury: "Today, Lisa is a very sick thirteen-year-old girl. We know that because of her damaged kidneys, she will be wedded to a kidney machine for the rest of her life. Three times a week she will undergo the ordeal of dialysis, for the rest of her life. This is the way she must live, if she is to live. Why is Lisa in this terrible predicament? Is it anything she did? Is it because she didn't seek medical care? Is it because she was neglected by her family, her mother, her father, her teachers? Why is she in this condition? This is the question for you to consider. You have heard the medical evidence, and you **know** why she is in this terrible condition. You know why she will be in this condition for the rest of her life. You know what happened to her because you have heard it, not from the attorneys or from the medical experts or from the medical records. You have heard the answer from Lisa's own treating physicians, Dr. Blade and Dr. Smith. You have heard her treating physicians testify as to their treatment plan, what tests they performed, and what their diagnosis was. You have heard her own doctors tell you that if she had a positive urine study, it could be medically significant. Her own treating doctors told you that she tested positive. That would be a sign of protein in her kidney, a sign that she had a kidney infection that had to be treated. This is about a long-term kidney infection she had over six years which was never diagnosed by her treating doctors, Dr. Blade and Dr. Smith, who told you that if you find a positive urine study, it is a definite sign of kidney failure and requires referral to a kidney specialist. Was Lisa ever found to have a positive urine study? Did her dip stick studies ever test positive?

"Yes! They did! We know she tested positive for these studies over several years! After her studies tested positive, was she referred to a nephrologist or to a hospital for treatment? We know she never was referred to a nephrologist. You have seen the actual test results. The tests were done at Savin Medical. These tests were ordered and supervised by Dr. Smith and Dr. Blade. The first positive test should have resulted in a referral. Shouldn't the second, third, fourth, over many years? Both doctors testified that it would be a violation of the standard of care, considering these positive studies over many years, not to refer Lisa to a kidney specialist. We do not need experts to say that. The defendants themselves have testified to that. Don't you believe them? Can't we take them at their word?"

Suddenly, Attorney Howe shouted like a thunderbolt in the silence of the night, "Judge, objection! May I approach the bench?" He screamed, "Mr. McArthur is deliberately misstating the evidence, as usual!" Judge Taylor, his face redder than ever, barked, "Mr. McArthur, I will have no one misstating evidence in my court. Approach the bench immediately!" Sean, shaken by this vicious and disturbing interruption, tried to calm down as he approached the bench. He knew the interruption was a deliberate attempt, preplanned by Howe, to disrupt his rhythm, throw off his timing and confuse the jury. Howe knew every trick in the book and he was using them artfully.

Howe: "Your Honor, the defendants testified as to what would be a violation but never admitted that they violated the standard." Judge Taylor, now in a very loud and hostile voice that could be heard not only by the jury but by everyone in the back rows of the courtroom: "You're right, Mr. Howe. Mr. McArthur, you are deliberately misstating the plaintiff's case. You know we do not have the transcripts and you're taking advantage of that. This is not my recollection. I recall that the defendants said they used their best judgment. That's what I recall them saying. Why don't you just admit that to the jury. Why don't you tell them that they tried to use their best judgment. You don't say that. You're trying to hoodwink this jury. You're not going to get away with this in my court. Anymore misleading arguments and I'll have the jury disregard your entire closing and I'll indicate that you do not have the credibility to stand before them and give them an honest charge. Do you get my drift?"

Sean knew that Howe and Taylor were not correct, that they were deliberately distorting the actual evidence. No matter what he said Sean's protest would have the effect of a raindrop in the burning desert. The clock that Judge Taylor had set for fifteen minutes was ticking away. Every minute, every second, Sean was at the bench was a minute or second subtracted from his allotted time. Things were now desperate. Another Howe or Taylor interruption would completely destroy Sean's credibility in front of the jury. He knew he was down to his last moments. He had no more legal capital he could afford to waste. Taylor was glaring at him, which meant that he was ready to interrupt if he had the chance. There was no way that Taylor or Howe would allow Sean to continue without further interruption. Sean knew he had to end his closing on a high note. But, how would he do it?

The case hung in the balance. Sean surveyed the jury once more. To his surprise, they were looking back with warmth in their eyes. For the first time, Sean felt that the jury actually felt empathy for him and for Lisa. The jury knew that Sean had not misstated the case and that Judge Taylor's harangue had been out of context. They understood the evidence. The defendants, Dr. Smith and Dr. Blade, did, in fact, admit in open court, in a very dramatic way in cross-examination, that they had not followed up positive findings, and they had conceded that a failure to do so would be a violation of the standard of care. They had admitted that a failure to follow up would cause Lisa to get an infection. That was undisputed. Howe's tactic had backfired as had Judge Taylor's uncontrollable harangue. Rather than losing credibility with the jury, Sean had actually gained it, in spades. Sean knew his last words had to be quick and on target. He studied each member of the jury, looking into their eyes and hearts for the last time. "You have heard all the evidence, it is compelling. Do justice, and God bless you."

Sean, drained, staggered to his seat. He wondered if he had successfully argued Lisa's case? He knew only time would tell. What happened next was a blank in Sean's mind. He had no recollection of Judge Taylor giving his usual pro-defense charge of "the defendants are to be judged by the standard of reasonable care giving the doctors the benefit of the doubt, if there is doubt." If the jury believed these pro-defense words, of course, the case was lost.

Sean wondered would the jury give the doctors the benefit of the doubt or would they give Lisa any benefit of the doubt? Wide judgment and benefit of the doubt were, in Sean's mind, an excuse to practice bad medicine. Could one use poor judgment and not violate the standard of care? Sean knew it would be a close call. Like all trial attorneys, he had no control over what the jury would do. He prayed to himself that the jury would remember the evidence and not be misguided by Howe's selective emotional closing which, in effect, asked the jury to find for the doctors because they were good doctors trying to help people. Judge Taylor's closing and instructions to the jury not only confused Sean but probably confused the jury as well. His boring monotone went on for over two hours. At the end of the instruction Sean could see the jury was mentally and physically exhausted.

Late in the day the jury was finally given the case. As the last juror left the courtroom, Judge Taylor slammed the gavel angrily, gave one last poisonous glance at Sean, one last smile to Howe, abruptly rose from his bench, and raced out. Sean shook Ed's hand and thanked him, as always, for his help and encouragement. He then went to his clients, nearly hidden in the back corner of the courtroom. He hugged the Rowes, kissed Lisa warmly on the forehead and gave her a hug, "All we can do now is pray. The case is in the hands of God, and an unpredictable Massachusetts jury."

Chapter 21

The Verdict

After only one hour of deliberation, the jury returned the largest medical verdict in the history of Massachusetts – Lisa won her case. The jury ruled against all three defendants in an amount over $30 million. With interest, the total verdict came to $45 million. Lisa's long-term medical, hospital, transplant, and dialysis expenses would be covered.

The verdict was also one of the largest in the country and it received substantial national TV coverage, and was discussed in medical and legal journals. The "Mecca of Medicine" in Massachusetts, and the medical establishment, was stunned. Conservative Massachusetts never had a multi-million dollar medical verdict so high.

The local papers featured bold headlines analyzing the negligent and dangerous practices of Savin Medical, and the need for pediatricians to stop using the dip stick tests.

Who would have thought that a brave thirteen-year-old girl would bring the medical profession to its knees and cause it to revise its entire medical procedure for testing and evaluating kidney disease? Even staunch media critics of malpractice cases, who had frequently attacked what they termed "frivolous medical cases," were happy that Lisa had won her case and that bad medicine was dealt a blow in the process.

Chapter 22

The Aftermath

The repercussions of the trial and of the significant verdict changed many people's lives. After the trial, Judge Taylor suffered a stroke while striking his gavel the day before he was to hear Attorney Howe's Motion for New Trial. Upon his death, Elizabeth Martinez, a newly appointed Hispanic trial judge and an honor graduate of one of the inner-city law schools, expeditiously denied the motion by all of the defendants for a new trial.

Lisa's case was quietly settled with the defendants' insurance carrier for the full amount of the verdict.

Dr. Hamilton continues his illustrious medical career and was recently voted one of the most outstanding nephrologists in the country. He wrote the current leading book on pediatric nephrology. He and Paula Murphy, Lisa's schoolteacher, were married a year after the verdict. They met and became more than good friends after the trial. Sean could tell when they first met that they would be the perfect couple.

Dr. Smith continued to practice medicine. He was appointed president of his local medical society and later became one of the highest paid lobbyists for the State Medical Society. He eventually was indicted by the Internal Revenue Service for income tax fraud and numerous violations of the Conflict of Interest law. He now resides in a government facility.

Dr. Blade continued his medical career, eventually becoming a leading investor, then owner of several large for-profit HMOs in the New England area. He frequently appears on national television as a strong medical advocate against any changes in patient's rights bills that would allow legal actions against HMOs that would change the measly $20,000 legal cap for suing hospitals in Massachusetts. His wife divorced him after his well-publicized affair with a summer intern, winning one of the highest alimony settlements in Massachusetts.

Lisa went on to have a kidney transplant from her mother. She studied medicine, became a pediatrician, and presently practices pediatrics in Boston. She is also on the staff of Pediatric Hospital and works closely with Dr. Hamilton.

Attorney Chauncy Howe still actively practices law. His name had been submitted to the judicial conference for an appointment and he was being considered to replace Judge Taylor, but his strong advocation of no-fault medical malpractice legislation makes his appointment by the liberal democratic controlled Governor's Council very doubtful. Attorney Howe also broke up the law firm he partnered with his brother over a bitter dispute concerning profits. This caused the split-up of one of the oldest law firms in Boston. The repercussions are still being felt throughout the legal community.

Quigley left the practice of law and is now the owner and manager of several pubs in London and Sydney. Whenever he returns to Boston, he always manages to get his photograph on one of the society pages of the Boston Globe.

Rosie continues to practice law and lectures frequently "to the bar" on how to win the "big case." He was recently named chief legal counsel to the National Airline Stewardesses Association and enjoys his many frequent flyer miles, travelling the world on their behalf.

After the case was settled, Sean left the three M's and gave up the practice of law for a year. During that time he gained some financial independence, pursued his interest in pediatric kidney research, and engaged in fundraising for Pediatric Hospital. He continues to work closely with Dr. Hamilton and his wife, Paula, sponsoring kidney research and fundraising efforts in Massachusetts and throughout the nation. After his sabbatical he returned to trial practice and has been engaged in many leading medical malpractice cases. He occasionally teaches law at Boston College Law School and his firm devotes one-third of its practice to doing pro bono work for medical causes for consumer groups. He has become a prolific writer and his novels on legal medical matters are sold throughout the United States.

Years after the verdict, things have returned to normal. Trial lawyers in Massachusetts still are frequently attacked in the press for bringing and trying too many medical malpractice cases.

The medical malpractice society, and its powerful insurance and physicians lobby, continues to bring bills before the legislature advocating no-fault medical malpractice. A national medical study recently was published by the Institute of Health pointing out that each year in the United States there are over 100,000 documented deaths that can be attributed to hospital or physicians' errors. These cases are not often pursued by the families of victims and until this study they went unnoticed. Medical errors and the mercenary pursuit of the financial bottom line by national and state-wide HMOs continue to weaken the quality of medical care throughout the United States. National legislation had to be enacted by Congress to allow women to stay in the hospital for two days rather than one day in order to prevent unnecessary medical risks to them and their babies. The war continues in the courtroom and, unfortunately, a little is being lost each day.

In Massachusetts, it is more difficult than ever to win a medical case; ninety percent of all medical cases recently tried in Massachusetts before a jury were lost. Massachusetts is in the unenviable position of standing 45th in the country for disciplining and suspending incompetent doctors.

Sean, in a prologue to one of his recent novels stated, "Unfortunately, in court, bad medicine still seems to prevail. In Massachusetts, medical insurers and the medical profession spend millions of dollars to defend bad medicine rather than advance and promote good medicine. What misplaced priorities! Will it take another verdict like Lisa's to shake and awaken the public? When will we learn from the mistakes of the past? Will we ever receive high quality medical care in this country, or will we be always shortchanged?"

When Sean feels low, he often thinks of his friend: "What encouraging words would Ed have at this time?" Every time Sean tried in court, he thought of his favorite clerk, Ed, and how he had done so much to help win Lisa's case. He was the real hero. His integrity truly won the day and saved the critical evidence from being tampered with or destroyed. Ed died in a car accident a few days after Sean had successfully opposed Howe's Motion for a new trial. Sean remembers Ed's last words that morning: "Sean, Amigo, you lucked out on this one. You finally had a good judge. Taylor has gone to his just reward. Let's hope we never see his likes again. Just one last word to you. I know you'll be taking some time off and I probably won't see you again for quite a while. Never forget what makes a great trial lawyer. No matter when, where, or how he's trying his case, trial lawyers persevere; they never give up; they fight for their client to the end. You don't know it because you're too close to it but, what made you a great trial attorney on Lisa's case is that you never gave up; you fought to the end. That's what I recognized in you, Sean. You don't give up and you **do** fight for your client, whatever the odds. When I see you in court, I think of what I could have been. But, you know, Sean, I have no regrets. I get more of a kick of helping lawyers like yourself on the sidelines, giving them that extra lift, that little encouragement they need when everything goes wrong. You know, Sean, sometimes, if you can't be a great player, there's nothing wrong with being the dedicated coach. Don't you agree, amigo?" Sean looked Ed right in the eyes as he always did, as he so respected and admired him, and said, "Without you, Ed, that case couldn't have been won."

James P. McCarthy

Every time Sean enters a courtroom, he looks at the ornate walls and sees intimidating, serious self-portraits of senior judges who have presided over trials in Massachusetts over the last hundred years. Each time he sees these portraits of judicial figures, he can't help thinking there's one portrait missing and he always sees it in his mind's eye. That's the portrait of Ed. Real heroes go unrecognized.